"Are you listening?" she asked.

"Sure. Why wouldn't I be?"

"I want you to understand what we're up against, and I'm going to talk fast so we can go back inside and get some sleep. Agreed?"

"I'm ready for bed." Not a lie. In his opinion, going to bed was an excellent idea that didn't necessarily include sleep.

"Here goes."

She spewed a torrent of data—including names, dates and amounts of cash payments—showing how Waltham had arranged with state police and ICE officials to open a corridor for a Mexican cartel. Though Blake didn't know much about how drugs were packaged and shipped, he had a high level of expertise when it came to weaponry. If Jordan's figures were correct, these semiautomatic guns, grenades and rocket launchers were enough to supply a small army.

"Wait." He held up his palm, halting this gush of information. "You've got plenty of evidence. Did you inform a prosecutor?"

"There are a couple of problems."

ESCAPE FROM ICE MOUNTAIN

—

USA TODAY Bestselling Author

CASSIE MILES

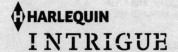

HARLEQUIN
INTRIGUE

To my Salem family, Marya Hunsinger and Dave McConnell,
a mystery-solving maven and a skier extraordinaire.
And, as always, for Rick.

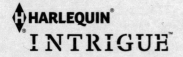

HARLEQUIN®
INTRIGUE™

ISBN-13: 978-1-335-58221-8

Escape from Ice Mountain

Copyright © 2022 by Kay Bergstrom

PLEASE RECYCLE

THIS PRODUCT IS RECYCLABLE

Recycling programs
for this product may
not exist in your area.

For questions and comments about the quality of this book,
please contact us at CustomerService@Harlequin.com.

Harlequin Enterprises ULC
22 Adelaide St. West, 41st Floor
Toronto, Ontario M5H 4E3, Canada
www.Harlequin.com

Printed in U.S.A.

Cassie Miles, a *USA TODAY* bestselling author, lived in Colorado for many years and has now moved to Oregon. Her home is an hour from the rugged Pacific Ocean and an hour from the Cascade Mountains—the best of both worlds—not to mention the incredible restaurants in Portland and award-winning wineries in the Willamette Valley. She's looking forward to exploring the Pacific Northwest and finding mysterious new settings for Harlequin Intrigue romances.

Books by Cassie Miles

Harlequin Intrigue

Visit the Author Profile page at Harlequin.com.

CAST OF CHARACTERS

Jordan Reese-Waltham—The former investigative reporter goes on the run to rescue her twin sons from her criminal ex-husband.

Blake Delaney—The Marine Corps captain who recently suffered a career-ending injury joins Jordan, his former lover, to bring her twins to the safety of his cabin on Ice Mountain.

Cooper and Alex Waltham—Jordan's five-year-old twin sons.

Hugh Waltham—Jordan's ex-husband is running for the Senate. His possible crimes include fraud, smuggling, money laundering and...murder.

Ray Gruber—As head of security, Ray is vicious in pursuit of Hugh Waltham's enemies.

Caspar Khaled—Owner of Magic Lantern Casino and known associate of Hugh.

Emily Finnegan—Former Las Vegas showgirl who runs a sightseeing helicopter service.

Chester Prynne—Blake's mentor, who also lives on Ice Mountain.

Chapter One

Timing was everything. In the next fifty-five minutes, Jordan Reese-Waltham would be on her way to freedom with her twin sons. Her countdown began when she was in the kitchen of the stucco, tile and flagstone mansion in the forested hills outside Flagstaff, Arizona. For almost five years, she'd shared this palatial home with her ex-husband, Hugh Waltham, and she'd learned everything about the property—details that were vital to the success of her mission.

At 7:34 p.m., Jordan stepped away from the chopping block, wiped her eight-inch stainless steel knife and slipped the razor-edged blade into a leather sheath. On the opposite side of her belt, she carried another holstered weapon: an expandable, titanium baton that opened to twenty-six inches and could be lethal when used properly in martial arts, which was one of her most well-practiced skills. Also, she was a decent chef—good enough to pose as a caterer.

Exiting the kitchen, she carried a platter of savory hors d'oeuvres into the ballroom. Her uniform—white shirt and black slacks—included a puffy chef toque over her curly brown hair, a gray pin-striped apron and the black surgical mask required for the catering staff. A decent disguise. Not that she'd be recognized at this posh event. The guests in attendance seldom paid attention to the help.

It was 7:36 p.m., which meant she had ten minutes to scan the ballroom, entryway and staircases to assess potential threats. She set her platter on a linen-covered buffet table, adjusted her thick woven leather bracelets and began fussing with other bits of food. As far as she could tell, nothing had changed in the lavish decor. All of it—the crystal chandeliers, gold-filigreed sconces and marble floors—still made her uncomfortable with its over-the-top display of wealth.

Tonight's event was a fundraiser to kick off Hugh's campaign for the US Senate. The ostentatious setting was appropriate for men in tailored suits carrying cash-heavy wallets and bejeweled women draped in designer gowns. Once, she'd been one of them.

Jordan positioned herself to see the entry foyer where Hugh stood beside his fiancée, Helena. His security chief, Ray Gruber, observed those who were entering. Gorilla Gruber had long arms, heavy shoulders and a sloping forehead like a Neanderthal. He looked relatively civilized in his three-piece suit, but she knew he was a monster. Three months and six days ago, he'd nearly killed her. His assault was called a suicide attempt and landed her in a mental health institute under lock and key. Someday, she'd get even with Gruber. But not tonight.

For the sake of her children, she needed to stay on schedule. It was 7:39 p.m. As she expected, the gracious, curving staircase to the left of the doorway was guarded and cordoned off with a velvet rope. More security guards were stationed throughout the ballroom.

At the end of a serving table, three stunning, classy ladies had gathered. Their smiles were uncomfortable. Their glances, furtive. Jordan suspected they were talking about her. After adjusting her mask, she edged closer to eavesdrop on her former associates—political wives.

The tallest was a former, one-named supermodel, Sierra, who would never admit to being over thirty. She flipped her long, auburn hair and said, "I guess none of us have heard from Jordan. She's been in the Gateway Institute for over three months. Does that sound about right?"

"I just don't understand why a woman who seems to have everything—a handsome husband, beautiful house, tons of money and healthy twin boys—would attempt suicide."

"I never thought she was suicidal. My friend was brave and strong," Abigail said, quick to defend Jordan. "When she was working full-time before the kids were born, she was a respected journalist, embedded with the troops in combat zones in the Middle East. She covered politics in the US House of Representatives."

"Which was where she met Hugh," Sierra added.

"But he's not a congressman," said the trophy wife. "Not like my hubby."

"Wake up, sweetie." The model sneered. "Hugh is a consultant for several of our husbands. He gets our boys elected, and he's more powerful and connected than any of them."

"Is that why he dumped Jordan? Trading her in for a newer model?"

"She did the dumping," Abigail said. "Jordan moved out over a year ago with the kids. I always thought she should have married a guy she got close to a long time ago when she reported on the troops. A far better man than Hugh Waltham. A marine with chiseled abs and the sweetest dimples."

Standing by a basket of fresh-baked breads, Jordan stiffened. *Stop talking, Abigail.* She didn't want her friend to mention Blake Delaney. He was essential to her escape plans, and she needed to downplay the connection between them.

Abigail continued, "I only met him once and never forgot the way he looked at her. If he knew Jordan was in the hospital, he'd be here at her side."

Nervous, she fidgeted. *Am I going to have to shove a baguette down Abigail's throat to make her be quiet?*

Sierra interrupted. "I never cared for Jordan's hard news. I liked it better when she did those cute undercover assignments, like when she pretended to be a chef or a stuntwoman or a fashion designer."

"Fluff pieces." Abigail scoffed. "Not worthy of her talent."

Jordan appreciated the compliment. Though they came from different generations, Abigail counted as one of her best friends.

"She's been in the Institute for months," said the trophy wife. "What's really wrong with her?"

"I heard she had other mental problems," said Sierra.

Jordan looked away from the conversation. Absently, she twisted her bracelets. Hugh was a master manipulator. He'd turned everything to his advantage, building a platform for his candidacy as a mental health advocate and using Jordan as an example of how the current system had failed.

His buddy, Dr. Stephen Merchant, ran the Institute where she'd been incarcerated, drugged and misdiagnosed. As soon as she got her kids safely away from Hugh, she'd find a way to expose Hugh, Dr. Merchant and all their cronies.

After one last scan of the ballroom, she returned to the kitchen and glanced down at the wristwatch above her bracelet. Her time was 7:46 p.m., right on schedule for the next phase of her plan. Since the front staircase was cordoned off and guarded, she needed a different access to the second-floor bedroom shared by her twins. The back stairway from the kitchen was locked. Picking it would arouse suspicion, but Jordan knew another route.

With a wave to the guy who had hired her to work for him as a caterer, she signaled that she was slipping out for a smoke. Once outside, she removed the mask. The October temperature was in the low fifties with a crisp, piñon pine–scented breeze. During the years she'd lived here, she'd explored every inch of the mansion and surrounding grounds. The place held no secrets from her, and she doubted that her ex-husband had changed anything. Why should he? This was *his* house. Everything suited him.

She circled the glass-enclosed turquoise swimming pool and ran to a gardener's shed hidden in the trees at the edge of the forest where she peeled off her caterer's outfit that was too white and bright for stealth. Underneath, she wore black leggings and a fitted, black, nylon hoodie. She stuffed the apron, toque and shirt into a backpack that she'd take with her so her friend in the catering business wouldn't get in trouble. Wearing a second backpack she'd stashed here earlier, she put on black gloves and darted through the night like a fleeting shadow.

At the far end of the house, she climbed a rose trellis as she'd done many times before. Several feet off the ground, she reached toward the window to the bathroom that adjoined the twins' bedroom and prayed that security hadn't noticed the window lock that had never fastened properly. She was in luck. The lock twisted and the window opened. After getting her balance on the ledge, she lowered herself inside.

Her watch read 7:58 p.m. *Perfect timing.* Whenever she and Hugh entertained, they made a point of coming to the twins' bedroom at exactly eight o'clock to tuck them in. Even though she wasn't here to remind him, he'd probably follow that routine.

Silently, she opened the bathroom door a crack so she could hear what was happening in the bedroom. The boys were talking about superheroes. The last time she'd seen them—when their father brought them to the Institute to show them that it was a lovely place with marble sculptures and a garden—Jordan had been drugged into a near stupor. It was all she could do to keep from collapsing.

Now, she was a different person, alert and revitalized. The sweet sound of her children's voices echoed in her ears with perfect harmony, even though they were arguing.

"It's way better to be super strong," said Alex. "If

anybody gets in your way, you can punch them in the nose."

"I'd rather turn invisible," said Cooper, who had been a Harry Potter fan since birth. "And cast magic spells."

"You're a butthead."

"If I had a magic wand, I'd make you into a frog."

"Frogman," Alex said. "I'd swim faster than a shark."

Jordan's chest swelled with pride. Her sons were not only smart, but they were funny. She could hardly wait to wrap her arms around them. Their bedroom door opened with a click, and she stiffened, preparing herself to hear Hugh's voice.

Instead, the sound was high-pitched and feminine. "How are my two favorite guys?"

"I'm fine, Helena." Alex was only five years old but managed to sound gruff. "You're wearing my mom's necklace."

"Gosh, I don't think so." Hugh's fiancée gave a twittering laugh. "Does it look good with my dress?"

"How should I know?" Alex muttered.

"Will you help me?" Cooper sounded friendlier. "Will you deliver a letter? In person."

"Sure thing, cutie-pie."

"This is important," Cooper said. "It's for Mom. I've sent her about a million letters, and she never answers. I don't think she's getting her mail."

Jordan hadn't seen a single note from either of the twins, and it was safe to assume that the letters she'd sent to them hadn't been delivered. No doubt, Dr. Merchant had cut off that possible communication. She had had no visitors, no telephone privileges and no access to a computer. They had wanted to keep her isolated.

But she'd figured out how to get around the restrictions and tap into the Institute's internet system, where she connected to the underground network used in her reporting.

"I'll give her the letter," said Helena. "Did you boys take your pills?"

"Why doesn't Mommy write back?" Jordan heard the pain in her son's voice. He continued, "Did she forget about us?"

"Your mother," said Helena, "is very sick. Don't think about her, okay?"

"Where's Dad?" Alex demanded.

"He's very busy, but he sends a hug and a kiss. Get into bed."

"I want a story," Cooper said. "Read to us."

"Sorry, boys. I've got to go."

Another voice joined the conversation. "I'd be happy to read something."

Abigail! What on earth was she doing here? Jordan held her breath. She hadn't planned for this interruption. There wasn't time. The clock was ticking, and she had to be out of the house with the boys before half past eight when the security team would make their hourly sweep of the grounds. At 8:09 p.m., there were only twenty-one minutes left.

"Thanks, Abigail," Helena snapped. "But I don't need your help."

"I'm not here for you." When she tried, she could put the authority of age into her voice. Helena didn't stand a chance against her. Abigail said, "Come here, boys."

Jordan heard her sons jumping out of bed and rushing to Abigail. There were happy sounds of laughter, babbling and snuggles. Desperately, Jordan wanted to be in that room, wanted to hug them, kiss them and rub her cheek against their soft brown hair.

"That's enough," Helena said. "I need to get back to the fundraiser."

"Sorry if I disturbed you," Abigail said. "I remembered that Hugh and Jordan always came upstairs at eight o'clock to tuck the boys in, and I wanted to see them."

"Now you have. Let's go."

"Sure thing. But first I need to go to the bathroom."

Jordan heard Abigail's voice coming closer and ducked behind the shower curtain before her friend stepped inside, flicked on the light and closed the door. "Jordan, are you in here?"

She pulled aside the curtain. "How did you know?"

"Did you really think I couldn't see through your disguise?"

She pulled Abigail into a hug. "No time to talk."

"Tell me what I can do to help."

"I don't want you involved," Jordan said firmly. "Hugh and Gruber are dangerous. The best thing you can do is walk away."

Abigail ran water in the sink and flushed the toilet. "I've been in touch with Blake. He's back from the Middle East."

Stunned, Jordan couldn't believe what she'd heard. "Why?"

"When you were eavesdropping, you must have heard what I said about Blake. He was worried when he couldn't get ahold of you. Finally, he contacted me."

"Go. Read to the boys. I'll join you in a minute."

When Abigail closed the bathroom door, Jordan sank onto the closed toilet seat. *Blake was worried about her.* Over the years, she'd thought of him so many times. If she had believed in soul mates, he would be hers. But their relationship hadn't worked seven years ago. They'd both been too dedicated to their careers.

Listening to the voices from the bedroom, she heard Helena leaving as Abigail settled down to read *The Hobbit*. The time was 8:13 p.m. Jordan had to go now, right now. But she hesitated.

Blake was back in the States. His unexpected arrival could ruin everything. Her plan had been to take the twins to Blake's cabin in Colorado where she'd once spent five amazing days with him. Since he was supposed to be stationed overseas, his house ought to be vacant. No one would think to look for her there. But now…

Fear surged through her veins. For the first time tonight, she doubted her ability to pull off this escape. So many things could go wrong. An orderly at the Institute could notice she was gone from her bedroom. The car she'd hidden at the edge of the property might be found and towed. Hugh's security staff, led by Gorilla Gruber, could catch them.

But she couldn't leave her boys here. Couldn't stop now.

She slipped through the door from the bathroom into the dimly lit bedroom where both of her sons were in their beds. Jordan placed a finger across her lips, signaling silence as Abigail stopped reading. Keeping her voice low and calm, Jordan said, "You have to be very quiet. Nobody can know what we're doing."

Kneeling, she held out her arms. Alex threw off his covers and bounded toward her. His skinny arms clamped around her with surprising strength. Cooper was less aggressive. He nestled close and whispered, "I knew you didn't forget us. I knew you'd come back."

After a handful of kisses, she issued orders to the boys. "Don't bother changing clothes. Put on your shoes and jackets. Throw some jeans and T-shirts in your backpacks. Do it fast."

Like little energy balls, they burst into action.

She turned to Abigail. "Are there guards posted outside the bedroom?"

"Only one. I'll distract him."

"And then, you'll forget you ever saw me. I mean it. I don't want you to get hurt."

"How are you getting out?"

"I'll take the boys across the landing to the back stairway."

"If I wasn't here, what would you have done?"

"I'm armed." Jordan patted her expandable, martial arts baton. "But I'd rather not use violence in front of the kids."

Abigail slipped out the bedroom door and went directly to the security guard. Though Jordan couldn't hear her conversation, she could tell that her friend was apparently claiming that she felt sick and needed help. The guard escorted her down the hallway to the staircase.

The time was 8:21 p.m. Nine minutes until the security sweep at the half hour. She drew the boys close to her. "We're going downstairs into the basement, then outside. Are you okay?"

"Tired," Cooper said, rubbing his eyes.

"Did you take the pills Helena gave you?"

Cooper nodded while Alex said, "No way. I don't like being sleepy."

"Try to keep up, boys. Be quiet, like ninjas."

After crossing the landing, they reached the stairway that descended to the kitchen level and then below it. In the basement, a single bulb lit the corridor. Years ago, she'd explored down here and remembered the layout. The wine cellar was in a room to the right.

Jordan went left through darkened rooms used for storage. Though tired, Cooper gamely followed, stumbling with every other step. Alex was bright-eyed and energetic, darting beside her like a small, nocturnal creature.

When she pushed open the door leading to the backyard, she used moonlight to check her wristwatch. It was 8:27 p.m. In three minutes, it would be too late.

She lifted Cooper into her arms. "Stick with me, Alex."

Together, they ran to the gardener's shed. When they ducked inside, the lights in the backyard burst into full illumination displaying the well-tended landscaping. Had they made it?

From the corner of her eye, she saw a man leaving the forest, coming out of nowhere. A tall, handsome marine wearing his dress blues. *Blake Delaney.*

He joined her in the shed and shut the door. Darkness surrounded them. For the first time in three months, she felt safe.

Chapter Two

Blake didn't ask why she was hiding in the garden shed with her twin sons. He didn't inquire about plans she'd made or weapons she was carrying. Instead, he closed the door to the shed behind himself and took charge of the situation. The apparent objective was to avoid being discovered by the security guards who were fanning out in the grounds behind the mansion. Before entering the shed, he'd counted five of them, which wasn't enough for a thorough sweep. No doubt if they found something suspicious, they could summon backup in seconds.

Inside the shed, the round October moon shone through a high window and gave enough light for him to see the two children and Jordan, who was even more striking than he remembered—beautiful, sexy and fierce as a mama grizzly. She pushed back her black hoodie, releasing an explosion of rich, chocolate-brown curls. Her enormous blue eyes stared up at him. Her full lips stretched in a grin as she extended her index finger and pointed to the gold-plated button in the center of his chest.

"You're a little bit overdressed," she said.

"Abigail's idea," he explained. "I didn't have an invite to this party, but a ranking marine in dress blues can get into almost any political gathering."

"I like the uniform." The moonlight made her look mysterious and seductive. "But there's no time for talk. We've got to—"

"I know." He interrupted and shushed her at the same time. "I got this."

He herded the little group to a far corner of the shed behind a riding mower and arranged lawn furniture to provide sufficient cover. When they ducked down, they couldn't be seen from the window or the door. In an almost silent voice, he said, "Stay here. Be quiet."

The boy Jordan had been carrying looked at Blake with wide eyes. "It's too dark."

Blake took out his key chain and detached a tiny LED flashlight. "Hold the light so nobody can see it from outside."

The other twin asked, "Are you a soldier?"

"Not exactly." He lifted his chin. "I'm a marine."

"You smell funny."

"My cigar."

Smoking the hand-rolled Havana, with its sweet, earthy aroma, had provided a good excuse for him to wander the grounds. As soon as he'd arrived at Waltham's place, his instincts had activated. This palatial home sure as hell didn't look like a fortified enemy stronghold, but the sense of danger was palpable. His suspicions had been confirmed moments ago when he got a text from Abigail. It said: Situation dire. Watch for J in backyard.

The spunky twin confronted him. "You shouldn't smoke."

Someday, the kid might understand the difference between a ceremonial cigar at the start of a mission and a bad habit. A discussion for another time. "No matter what you see or hear, remain hidden. Take care of your mom and brother."

"Okay."

Blake snapped a salute. "Give me a 'yessir.' Quietly."

"Yes, sir," the boy whispered.

Before he left them, Blake glided the back of his hand down Jordan's soft, pale cheek and patted her shoulder. In her blue eyes, he saw strength, courage and…hope? He could tell that she truly believed she could pull off this impossible scheme to save her kids. Strange but, God help him, he'd do his best to make that happen.

Behind the riding mower and the lawn furniture, they were well hidden, but he needed to create further distraction by drawing attention to himself. Straightening his gleaming white hat with the gold Marine Corps insignia, he slipped through the door and left the shed. He stayed in the shadows until he reached the rocky ledge where he'd abandoned his half-smoked cigar.

Though he wasn't carrying his M18 pistol or ceremonial sword, he was prepared for conflict. A few weeks ago, when he heard that Jordan was an inpatient at the Gateway Mental Health Institute, he'd been worried. Though he'd lost touch with Jordan, who was, after all, married to another man, he'd never stopped thinking about her, dreaming about what might have been if they both hadn't been so attached to their careers. *Not anymore, not for him.* Blake teetered at the edge of retirement, which was another reason he'd wanted to meet with Jordan. He had to find out if there was a chance for them, a possibility of a future together.

He'd tried calling, to no avail. Then he'd come to Flagstaff and had been stonewalled at every turn until he contacted her friend, Abigail, who told him that Jordan was being held at the Institute, not allowed to communicate with anyone. Abigail suggested meeting at this fundraiser, where he might be able to talk to Hugh Waltham, the ex-husband, and get a pass to see Jordan.

He fired up his Zippo and lit the fragrant Havana. About fifteen feet away from the door to the garden shed, he stepped onto the winding flagstone path that circled the enclosed swimming pool and led to a gazebo. It only took a few minutes for two of the security guards to approach.

Both were muscular, dressed in suits with white shirts and conservative neckties. Both wore earpieces with attached wires for communication. They strode confidently toward him. He guessed that the taller guard—almost equal to Blake's six feet four inches— was former military from his buzz cut and obvious respect for the uniform. The other guy had a broad chest, wide shoulders and long arms like an ape. His attitude of authority was unmistakable. The gorilla was the boss. He spoke first.

"What the hell are you doing out here?"

"Good evening, gentlemen." Blake tugged on his brim. Worn low on his forehead, his hat provided cover. "I'm enjoying a smoke. Wish I could offer you a cigar, but this bad boy is my last hand-rolled Havana."

The beanpole asked, "Were you stationed in Cuba, Captain?"

Definitely military—he'd recognized Blake's rank from the stripes on his sleeve and the two silver bars on his jacket. "I've been in and around the Middle East for the past decade or so."

"In combat?"

"Oorah."

That word cemented his credentials as a leatherneck marine, not a man to be treated with disrespect. Still, the Ape-Man squared off in a confrontational pose that he probably thought made him look bigger and tougher. Blake saw him as a larger target.

Gruffly, Ape-Man said, "Put out the cigar and go inside. The yard is off-limits."

Blake had to wonder why. Had there been threats? Had anyone gotten wind of Jordan's plan? He inhaled deeply and blew out a cloud of smoke as he turned toward the beanpole. "Where were you stationed?"

"On a carrier in the Pacific. The navy was a long time ago. Sometimes I miss it."

"I can tell you do." Blake turned to Ape-Man. "How about you?"

"Not that it's any of your damn business, but I never enlisted. I learned my skills on the street. I was a cop in Chicago."

"That can be a dangerous assignment." *If you're dumb enough to get into fights.*

"Damn right."

Ape-Man stuck out his square jaw. His squinty eyes fired a challenge. He was a boss and a bully…and a fool to think he could take a marine in hand-to-hand combat. Blake was seriously tempted to jab his knuckles into Ape-Man's face, ram a knee into his groin and tie his long arms into a square knot. But tonight wasn't about him. He needed to tone down his natural impulses, to think of Jordan and the twins. "Mind if I walk with you for a few paces?"

"No problem," said the beanpole. "Things have changed in the Middle East. What can you tell us?"

"I'm not a politician," Blake said. "I follow orders and try not to get into trouble. All I figured out is that the people are smart, generous and funny. And the food is great, especially shawarma and hummus."

As they continued talking, they walked past the garden shed without giving it a second glance. This distraction had been more successful than Blake thought possible. They were approaching the path that led to the gazebo when Ape-Man had a second thought. He snapped off an order to the beanpole. "Go back to that shed and take a look inside."

"Okay, I'm on it."

With surreptitious glances, Blake watched the tall, skinny security guard trot to the garden shed, pull open the door and stick his head inside. The obstacle course Blake had set up should be a deterrent to exploring, but he wouldn't relax until the guard called out an all clear. The greater threat came from Ape-Man. If that guy got his paws on Jordan and the kids, he'd do serious damage.

Blowing another puff of smoke, Blake spoke to the boss. "How many guards do you use for an event like this one?"

"More than a dozen."

"Why so many? Have there been threats?"

"You wouldn't understand," said the Ape-Man. "As

you already noted, you aren't a politician. These men have a lot of enemies."

"Have you worked for Hugh Waltham before?"

"I've been on the payroll for years." His squinty eyes turned dark and angry. "You ask a lot of questions."

"Just curious." Blake watched as the beanpole closed the door to the shed and came back toward them. He hadn't spotted Jordan and the kids. They were safe.

Ape-Man said, "If you're smart, you'll mind your own business."

With a sigh of relief, Blake stubbed out his cigar and turned away from the Ape-Man. "Have a good night, gentlemen. I'll see you inside."

As he strolled toward the front of the house, he wondered what had happened that made Hugh Waltham think he needed a full-time security staff. Had he made enemies? Or was he just paranoid?

At the end of the path, he ducked into the trees and foliage at the edge of the manicured lawn and returned to the garden shed. Crouched behind a rock, he watched the security patrol complete their rounds and return to the party. The last man to enter was the boss, who scowled as he scanned the entire yard and then nodded with satisfaction. Didn't suspect a thing.

The guy was blinded by overconfidence and not all that bright. He hadn't frisked Blake, hadn't noticed the bulge from his ankle holster, hadn't even asked for his name to check against the guest list. Not a genius. But still dangerous.

He slipped into the garden shed and went to the corner where Jordan and the kids were hiding. Both boys were awake. He gave them a two-fisted thumbs-up and whispered, "We're cool. The security guys are gone."

Jordan hugged her twins and released them with obvious reluctance. "We should go."

He agreed. As soon as the twins' disappearance was discovered, the security force would be more intense in their search and pursuit. "Where to?"

"I have a car hidden on the other side of the golf course," she said. "Follow me."

Blake eyed both twins. Cooper seemed to have recovered his strength—a side benefit of fear and adrenaline. Alex was okay for running on his own. If they needed help, Blake could carry either or both kids and their backpacks. He unbuttoned his jacket and stuck his hat inside, which would probably ruin it, but he couldn't be secretive while wearing a bright white hat.

Jordan stepped outside, followed by the twins, and Blake brought up the rear. Holding Cooper's hand, Jordan moved swiftly through the forested area beyond the house, dodging through stands of ponderosa pine, golden aspen and flat boulders that mimicked the plateaus and mesas of the high desert. This part of Arizona reminded him of Colorado, where he had a log cabin in the wilderness.

Jordan paused in the rough at the edge of a golf course with a green fairway that contrasted with the autumn foliage. Obviously, she and the boys had walked this way before. Quick and sure-footed, they covered a lot of ground in a minimum amount of time.

Her car, a Prius, awaited on a residential street beyond the golf course. With every step he took, Blake came up with another question. How had she escaped from the Institute? Where did she get the cash to finance this escape? Whose car was this?

While she helped the twins get belted into their booster seats in the back, he got behind the steering wheel and adjusted the seat for his long legs. Finished with the boys, she stood outside the driver's side window with her fists on her hips. "You're not driving, Blake."

"But I am," he said. "Our first stop has to be my motel so I can change clothes. I love my dress blues, but they're too obvious to blend in with the crowd."

"Why do you think you're coming with us?"

"You need me."

She didn't deny it. Instead, she circled the car and got into the passenger seat. "You have ten minutes to grab your stuff. After that, I'm driving, which only makes sense because I know where we're going."

When the little Prius pulled away from the curb, the surge of acceleration surprised him, but he missed the vroom-vroom sound of a regular engine. "Exactly where the hell are we going?"

JORDAN DIDN'T WANT to answer him. Having Blake as a partner gave her a boost of confidence, not to mention the obvious fact that she truly enjoyed looking at him, memorizing his high cheekbones and stubborn jaw. When he touched her, she catapulted back in time to when she was a giddy, young reporter, swept off her feet by a studly marine. However, having him show up wasn't all lollipops and rainbows.

First question: Could she trust him? He might feel compelled to turn her in to the authorities. No matter how justified, kidnapping her children violated federal law, especially since she intended to take them across state lines. Blake wasn't a lawbreaker.

Not like her ex-husband, who would be justified in calling in the FBI. She doubted he'd take that step. Hugh had been playing fast and loose with the law for many years and couldn't afford to have her tell all she knew. At least, she hoped he wouldn't call the feds. If the FBI got involved, there was a good chance she'd be caught. But she might be able to outsmart Hugh's private security team.

She tilted her head and looked up at Blake. "I guess I owe you an explanation."

"I guess so."

"It's complicated."

Her first objective in taking the twins was, of course, to rescue them from a life with Hugh and Helena that already included drugs at bedtime, tight controls and ultimately being shipped off to boarding school. In his way, Hugh loved the kids, mostly because they made photogenic props for campaign photos. But he'd never enjoyed playing with them or listening to them. From the moment she gave birth, Jordan had been the primary caregiver.

The boys were the most important thing in her life. In second place was her ongoing work as an investigative reporter. While on the run from Hugh, she intended to solidify her case against him, which was her primary reason for going on the run. Her ex was a crook, possibly a murderer, and she couldn't let him get away with any of his wrongdoing. After he assaulted her and had her locked away in the Institute, her investigation into his crimes had taken on more urgency.

Aware that she still hadn't responded to Blake's question, she twisted around and looked into the back seat. "How are you boys doing?"

"Good," Cooper said.

"You didn't answer Mr. Marine," the other twin said. "Where the hell are we going?"

"Language, Alex."

"Sorry, Mom."

"We're going on an adventure."

Blake cleared his throat. "I'm going to need more details."

"Don't worry. I planned strategically for this trip. Nothing has been left to chance."

"Every mission I've undertaken has taught me to expect the unexpected. For example, you didn't plan for me to join you."

"Definitely an issue, and I'll need to make adjustments," she said. "I knew it would be difficult to travel anonymously with adorable twin boys. Now I've got Thor driving the Prius."

He shot her a look that was probably supposed to be glowering. Instead, the laser gleam from his intense blue eyes set fire to a passion she hadn't felt in years. His deep voice rumbled. "You still haven't given me our destination."

Might as well get this over with. "When I first planned this trip, I wanted to go somewhere isolated, which made me think of your cabin in Colorado. I figured that you'd be stationed abroad and would never know that we moved in for a couple of weeks."

"You remembered our time at Ice Mountain."

"I think about it frequently."

"Smart choice, Jordan. My cabin comes equipped with the latest in security protection and has superinsulation for when it snows, which could happen soon."

"You don't mind?" she asked, with a slight hesitation.

"I'm honored."

"So, after you get your clothes from the motel, we'll go west on I-40."

He shrugged. "It's faster to go north on US-191 and hook up with I-70."

"But I don't want to make a beeline from Flagstaff to your place. We could be traced, tracked or followed. Our first stop needs to be a diversion."

"I agree with the logic but don't get too complicated. Where is this diversion?"

"Vegas."

Chapter Three

"Las Vegas is the opposite direction from our real destination," Jordan explained. "That's why we're going there."

"Tell me more," Blake said.

"We're setting a false trail, and Vegas would be the perfect place to establish that we're headed toward the coast. It's the sixth most heavily surveilled city in the country."

"What they say is *not* true." He grinned. "What happens in Vegas doesn't necessarily stay there."

With her head swiveled around like an owl, Jordan peered through the back window of the car to make sure they hadn't been followed into the parking lot of the Silver Stirrup Motel. The coast was clear. She watched as Blake glided the Prius into a space outside room twelve at the far end of the one-story rectangular building. Not an upscale place but she approved of the anonymity. At 9:24 p.m., she saw few cars in the lot, and the sidewalks outside the rooms were vacant. Nobody around. *Good news.* She didn't want to be noticed.

Before Blake got out of the car, she said, "You've got exactly ten minutes. We'll be timing you."

"Seriously?"

"I have a plan." According to her calculations, it would take almost four hours to reach Las Vegas. When they arrived, it would be around 1:30 a.m., and she had a lot to do between arrival time and departure. "I have a meeting scheduled at 3 a.m., and I can't be late."

After he snapped a quick salute, looking every inch a marine, he strode toward his motel room. She hadn't intended to have him with them on the trip but was glad things turned out this way. Blake provided much-needed protection from thugs like Gorilla Gruber and whatever else Hugh would throw at her.

She got out of the car, circled around to the driver's side and adjusted the seat, scooting forward for what seemed like a mile so her feet could reach the pedals. Then she turned her body so she could see into the back where the twins watched from their car seats. A glow from the motel lights reached into the car and showed confusion shining in their sweet blue eyes. They must have had questions but said nothing. Though proud of them for not freaking out, she felt a twinge of regret shudder through her. Once again, she'd introduced chaos into their lives. Her darling boys deserved an explanation for why their mommy had crept into their bedroom and carried them off into the night.

She passed her analog wristwatch with the extra-large numbers to Cooper, who was more diligent with his lessons and knew how to tell time. Actually, he enjoyed timing things. "Ten minutes," she said. "Tell me when it's up."

"You got it, Mom."

"Do you guys remember what happened about a year ago?" She kept her voice low and calm in spite of the anxiety that constricted her throat. "It was a night like this, with a million stars in the sky."

"An adventure," Cooper said. "Daddy was in Washington, and you took us to live in the little blue house with the tire swing."

"I liked it there," Alex said.

She agreed with him. In the family-oriented neighborhood, the twins had plenty of friends. Their lives without Hugh were blessedly normal. She reached between the seats and patted his knee. "We're going to live somewhere else for a while."

"Can we go back to school?" Cooper asked. "I miss the teachers."

She hadn't known they weren't enrolled in school. "What are you doing now?"

"A tutor," Alex said. "He's a dorkface."

"I promise to get you back into school as quickly as possible."

"Will Daddy be at our new home?" Alex asked.

"No." The pain of ripping their little family apart twisted in her gut. She hadn't wanted to be a single mother, but she'd brought this on herself when she'd been foolish enough to fall in love with Hugh Waltham and then to marry him. No excuses. And she wouldn't lie to her kids about getting back together with their father.

Alex had another question. "Are you divorced?"

"Yes."

She'd talked to the twins about divorce before the separation and had taken them for sessions with a child psychologist to help them deal with this complicated topic. "Your dad and I will never live together again, but that doesn't change how he feels about you. Your dad cares about you, and you'll be able to see him when you want to."

Alex blurted, "I don't like Helena. She wants me to call her 'mommy,' but I told her to go jump off a bridge."

Good for you. Though cheering inside, she knew better than to encourage hostility. "She's your dad's fiancée, so you should try to get along with her."

"Six minutes left," Cooper said. "What are you going to do if Blake doesn't make it in time?"

"What do you think I should do?"

"Spank him," Alex said. "Punch him in the nose."

"Again with the violence?" Blake would probably love to be spanked, but she definitely wasn't going to go there, not with the kids watching. "Have you been playing those psycho-killer video games again?"

"Dad said I could."

"Your father and I don't agree on that policy. Actually, there are a lot of things we think differently about." She gestured with her hands held wide. "The door is open. You can talk to me about absolutely anything."

Questions poured forth. Cooper wanted to change their bedtime to an hour later. Alex claimed they should be paid an allowance. Really? Wasn't five-almost-six too young? They both stated a need for cell phones. Before she could come up with detailed answers and rationales, Cooper had another announcement.

"Blake has one minute left," he said loudly.

"Do a countdown," Alex said. "Mommy won't let him get away with this. If he's not here, Mr. Marine is going to be in deep doo-doo."

She loved the way the boys considered her rules to be

law but didn't know how she could effectively discipline Blake. While the twins initiated their countdown, the door to Blake's room whipped open, and he stalked out, wearing cargo pants, a black T-shirt under a denim jacket and black sneakers. The uniform was gone, but he still looked like a strong, tough, impressive marine. He carried a duffel and a garment bag to the rear of the car. She popped open the trunk and he shoved his belongings inside.

"…three…two…one," the twins chanted as Blake slipped into the Prius and adjusted the passenger seat all the way back.

"Made it," he said.

"Lucky for you," Cooper said.

"Yeah," Alex jeered. "Mom was going to smack your bottom."

Blake raised an eyebrow. "Is that right?"

"Rules are rules," she said as she retrieved her watch from Cooper and fastened it to her wrist above her woven bracelet.

The time was 9:37 p.m., which was slightly more than two hours from the time she'd started her plan into motion. The twins had been missing from their bedroom for one hour and twenty-four minutes. If old patterns held true, the nanny would check on them at eleven—an hour and a half from now. Jordan needed to put significant distance between the Prius and Flagstaff before then. At 11:30 p.m., she'd call Abigail's cell phone using a super-encrypted phone of her own. She'd get an update from her friend and another chance to warn her not to tell anyone about seeing her or Blake. Abigail shouldn't be involved in this dangerous escape.

In just a few minutes, she maneuvered her little car

out of town and onto I-40, where she set her cruise speed at no more than five miles over the limit, which was seventy-five. The little Prius was flying. Though she tuned the radio to a low-key jazz station in the hope of lulling the twins to sleep, they'd caught the spirit of adventure and babbled energetically. Cooper wanted to know where they could go trick-or-treating at the end of the month and said he'd wear a Harry Potter costume, again. Alex repeated his need for an allowance and hinted that a hundred bucks a week would be cool.

While concentrating on the road, Jordan listened to the chatter with half an ear. Were they never going to be quiet and get some sleep? She glanced toward Blake and mouthed the words, *Help me*.

He gave her a grin and poked his head into the space between the seats so he could talk to the twins. "I know you guys are too grown-up for fairy tales," he said, "but I've got a war story you might appreciate. By the way, I've got intel on this very road we're driving on: Interstate 40. The nickname for this stretch through Arizona is Purple Heart Trail. Do you know what a Purple Heart is?"

"Some kind of medal," Alex said.

"You got it, kid. Warriors wounded in battle receive the Purple Heart. This highway celebrates those heroes."

Jordan spotted a road sign with the emblem for the Purple Heart and pointed it out. The kids craned to see.

"Have you got a Purple Heart?" Alex asked.

"Sure do." Blake spoke casually as though the medal wasn't an important honor. She knew better. He had two

Purple Hearts and a Medal of Honor. Captain Blake Delaney pretty much defined heroic. He had another question for the twins. "Do you know what a squad is?"

Alex launched into an answer that had something to do with football and didn't make a lot of sense. Cooper called him on his far-fetched explanation. "You don't know."

"Do too."

"Do not."

"Blake can tell us."

"The kind of squad I'm talking about," Blake said, "is part of a military platoon, which is usually about fifty people. Squads can have special assignments, like reconnaissance or providing medical aid or handling search and rescue operations. I've got a war story about the Tiger Squad."

"A true story?"

"You decide."

Blake had captured their attention. As he continued to talk in his low, soothing voice, the twins settled down to listen. With any luck they'd be asleep in minutes, and Jordan was anxious for that to happen. She needed time to talk to Blake without the kids listening. Thus far, he'd been an amazingly good sport, but she couldn't expect him to continue this journey without knowing what he was getting into.

He continued his story. "The main thing you've got to know about Tiger is that he's fierce. A striped, orange tomcat with a torn ear and a bent tail, he used to live with me in Colorado."

"A kitty?" Alex scoffed.

"Have you ever fought with a cat? Tiger could back down a grizzly bear. A ferocious cat who was afraid of nothing, Tiger led his squad to glory. Once he and his team rescued a five-year-old boy—same age as you guys—who discovered a treasure chest full of gold bars that had been hidden by outlaws in a mountain cave."

"I want to hear that story," Cooper said.

"First, let me tell you about the Rocky Mountains." Blake's voice dropped into a compelling rhythm. "Towering peaks with snow on top, crystal clear lakes and rushing rivers with white-water rapids. The red rocks form incredible shapes like sculptures. Granite boulders are the size of station wagons. You can ski, snowboard, hike and climb. Or sit in the sun under a clear blue sky and read a book."

His tone had a calming effect. Nothing bad could happen while Blake told his story. He was good with kids, which shouldn't have surprised her. Blake made a positive impression on practically everybody he met. But five-year-old boys could be especially difficult— rambunctious, headstrong and prone to getting into trouble. Not that her handsome twins would ever be described as brats.

She checked the time on her watch: 10:56 p.m. In just a few minutes, the nanny at Hugh's mansion would discover the twins were gone. And then…what? They'd made good progress, had already left the hill country surrounding Flagstaff and were driving fast on the two-lane, divided highway headed west through high desert.

Blake's voice went quiet, and she glanced toward him. "Are they asleep?"

"Couldn't keep their eyes open."

"Thanks for handling them."

"My pleasure," he said. "One of my favorite jobs was teaching at a reconstructed school in Qatar. Being around the kids reminded me why we were there. They're the future, especially the little girls."

She liked this side of his personality. Sure, Blake could be a badass marine, but he was also gentle and happy to help others. "While the boys are sleeping, I want to explain a few things and tell you how I was driven to kidnap my own children."

"I'm listening."

"Long story short, I discovered that Hugh was involved in bribery, extortion, money laundering and possibly worse crimes." They had argued but were never able to reach an understanding. He'd refused to step back and blow the whistle on the criminals he associated with. He'd told her he was in too deep. He'd be ruined. "We went back and forth, and he convinced me he was cleaning up his act. It was the opposite. His crimes got more serious. About a year ago, I packed up the twins and bought a cozy, little house in town."

"Question," Blake said. "How did you afford the move?"

"I always maintained separate savings, investments and checking accounts. Money that Hugh couldn't get his grubby hands on. I continued to work freelance after the twins were born and banked all my earnings. Also, after years of working full-time as a reporter and correspondent, I had built up a decent portfolio."

"I always knew you were a survivor."

"You bet I am," she said. "Back to my story… It's not as satisfying as your account of the Tiger Squad."

"But it really happened. That counts for a lot."

"About three months ago, Hugh made an appointment to see me and sign the final draft of a divorce agreement his lawyers drew up. I arranged for the twins to have a playdate, so I was alone in the house. When he arrived at my doorstep, I was immediately suspicious."

"Why?"

"He was accompanied by his chief of security, Ray Gruber. Why would he bring the muscle unless he was expecting trouble?" The memory of that afternoon caused her to tense. Her fingers tightened on the steering wheel. "We'd already discussed the terms for the divorce, but Hugh tried to sneak in one more clause, stating that he'd have sole custody of the twins."

"You refused to sign," Blake said.

"Damn right, I refused." She'd exploded, stormed through the house, yelling and cursing. "I told him and his bodyguard to get the hell away from me. I had my phone in hand and hit the call button for 911. I didn't have time to do anything more than scream hysterically at the emergency operator. My address—that was all I could get out. Gruber came toward me, zapped me with a stun gun and injected me with some kind of fast-acting sedative. I crumpled to the floor. As good as dead."

The aftermath was, in some ways, worse than death. She should have been smarter, should have been prepared for violence when she made the appointment with Hugh. She knew he'd do anything to get his way.

"When I regained consciousness for a moment, I

was being loaded onto a gurney. There was blood everywhere. My wrists had been slashed."

"The bracelets," he said. "I wondered why you were wearing them."

"Hugh explained to the paramedics that I had attempted suicide. Hours later, I woke up in Gateway Mental Health Institute. I had restraints at my wrists and ankles."

"Do you think Hugh meant to kill you?"

"I'm guessing that was the plan, but my call to 911 provoked the emergency response."

He reached toward her. With his large hand, he massaged the tight muscles at the base of her neck. "About this Gruber person, is he square-shaped with heavy shoulders and long arms? Built like an ape?"

"I call him Gorilla Gruber."

"Ape-Man," Blake said. "I met him outside the garden shed. If I'd known what he did to you, I would have taken a measure of revenge."

A measure of revenge? His phrase sounded civilized, but she knew his justified assault on the Gorilla would be ferocious. "You talked to him? Does he know who you are?"

"Ape-Man never asked for my name. He's not the brightest primate on the tree. And I never actually went inside the house and shook hands with your ex."

If Hugh initiated a search into her friends and associates, Blake's name might come up. "If Hugh and his minions have identified you, I might have to rethink my plan to go use your cabin as a hideout."

"The property isn't in my name. I bought it with

a friend who was killed in battle. His name is on the deed."

She glanced away from the straight ribbon of road illuminated by her brights and focused on him. "Is it a secret hideout? Do you think of the cabin as your Fortress of Solitude?"

"It's a place I can go when I need to be alone and lick my wounds. But I do have friends who live nearby and keep an eye on my belongings."

He had friends everywhere. Many were former marines he had served with and with whom he'd formed unbreakable bonds. Oddly enough, she had a similar network. In her work as an investigative reporter, she had developed friendships with smart people who could help her dig for the truth. One of those friends—a former showgirl who now ran a helicopter service—was waiting for her and the twins in Las Vegas.

"Did anybody else know you were in Flagstaff?"

"I paid a visit to the Gateway Institute, so a couple of the nurses might remember me. And, of course, I called Abigail."

"Speaking of my wonderful friend," she said. "It's 11:22. I'll give her a call and let her know we're all right."

"Do you have further plans with her?"

"Absolutely not. Too dangerous. I don't want her to get mixed up in this."

After they decided not to use the speakerphone because it might wake the kids, Blake punched in the number and held the cell so she could talk. Abigail answered immediately.

"I've only got a minute," she said. "If I didn't know you grabbed the boys, I wouldn't have guessed. Hugh is keeping the situation quiet. Not notifying the police or the FBI or anybody else."

Jordan expected this to happen. Though Gruber was a fool, her ex-husband was a mastermind who always thought several steps ahead. Hugh knew that she had damning information she could use against him and didn't want her talking to the authorities. "What is he telling people?"

"Something about the twins going on a vacation." Abigail paused. "He's sent Gruber to find you."

"How on earth did you figure this out?"

"When you get to be my advanced age, it's easy to fade into the woodwork, which means I'm great at eavesdropping."

Jordan had never intended to put her friend in this situation. Betraying Hugh was a dangerous game. She knew from personal experience that the stakes were high. "Be careful. Don't underestimate Hugh and his friends."

"I'll keep my distance from him. But Helena is my new best friend and can't wait to tell me everything."

After thanking Abigail, Jordan turned her attention back to the road. Nervous, she glanced toward Blake. "What do you think?"

"It's all good," he said. "If the feds had put out an alert for you and the twins, there's no way you could hide from them. You'd be arrested, charged with kidnapping and sent to prison. Ape-Man will be easier to fool."

That wasn't the biggest difference between legitimate law enforcement and Hugh's private security force. "If Gruber finds me, I won't be going to jail. He'll kill me."

Chapter Four

"I understand why you kidnapped the boys," Blake said, forcing himself to set aside his outrage at the way she'd been abused. "You can't work with your ex and can't talk to him. He's unreasonable, untrustworthy. And he is one hell of a dangerous individual."

She glanced toward the back seat. "Keep your voice down. I don't want the boys to hear about—"

"About how dear old Dad tried to kill you?"

"I try not to bad-mouth him to his sons. Whether I like it or not, they deserve a chance to have a relationship with their father."

Though he agreed with her in principle, she might need to release the fantasy that her ex would turn into a decent human being. Hugh Waltham, the successful political consultant, gave new meaning to the concept of sleazy self-interest. Apparently, Blake wasn't the only person who thought so. In his brief conversation with the ape who he now knew as Gruber, he'd learned that her ex had hired a team of bodyguards, which meant he had enemies.

He wondered if the threat to Waltham connected with the reasons Jordan had for separating from him and taking the kids and moving to a house in Flagstaff. In the glow from the dashboard, he studied the stubborn jut of her chin and her unswerving gaze on the road ahead. Seven years ago—when she'd been an embedded reporter, he had admired her bravery and her grit. No challenge had been too great. No threat too daunting. She'd thrown herself into every project, including those bivouacked nights when they made love in the open air.

Before he'd heard the details of her ex's assault on her, Blake had hoped to convince her to reconsider the kidnapping. She'd broken the law and the outcome of that desperate act could destroy her life. Aiding and abetting her on this mission didn't bode well for him, either. But he wasn't concerned about the consequences for himself. From the moment he saw her and the kids, he knew in the raw depths of his soul that he had to protect them.

He trusted her. His value system included firm belief in the rule of law, and he also believed in justice. Sometimes, the legal system failed. Separating the twins from their mother was flat-out wrong. Leaving them with her ex-husband? Worse.

"You haven't told me everything," he said.

She shrugged. "What do you want to know?"

When he first got to Flagstaff, he'd gone to the Gateway Institute where he'd heard she was a patient. The sprawling complex with several two- and three-story buildings covered several acres on the outskirts of town. The grounds featured immaculate grooming, colorful gardens and a pleasant array of paths for strolling. A valet had taken his car at the front entry, which made him expect cooperation, but he hadn't made it much farther than the reception counter, which was staffed by people in beige suits. The atmosphere reminded him more of an exclusive hotel than a facility for treating patients.

"The Gateway Institute," he said. "From what I saw, it's a classy place."

"Most of the inmates would agree. There are attractive common areas, a spa, a gym and dining areas with gourmet chefs. The level of care ranges from minimal assisted living to inpatient hospital care. If I had actually needed medical or psychiatric treatment, I might have chosen the Institute. But I wasn't sick."

"How did they keep you there?"

"Hugh's hotshot lawyers drew up the paperwork to have me committed, stating that I was a danger to myself and others. According to them, I couldn't be trusted with my twins."

"And that fooled the people at the Institute?"

"The legal petition was granted because the man in charge at Gateway, Dr. Stephen Merchant, is one of Hugh's cohorts. Once under his thumb, I was helpless. When I regained consciousness, I was drugged out of my mind."

"Why didn't you contact a lawyer or someone to help you leave?"

"Not possible. All my communications were cut." The corner of her mouth twisted in a bitter scowl. "Whenever I demanded my rights or showed signs of disobedience, I was locked in a windowless, padded room, sometimes in a straitjacket."

Blake had witnessed horrific mistreatment in military prisons and hostage situations, but he didn't expect to find similar tortures at a fancy spa tucked away in the mountains of Arizona. "How did you escape?"

"Lucky for me, I knew someone on the inside. I did an article on the Institute and their research on Alzheimer's. The woman who was my primary source recognized me and helped me out. She gave me access to a computer, and I plugged into my network of researchers. It took a while, but I worked out the details of paying cash and using a fake identity for the registration on this Prius—an excellent getaway car that's silent and seldom runs out of gas. I was able to contact a chef who helped me find work as a caterer at Blake's campaign party. A nurse at Gateway—who hates Dr. Merchant almost as much as I do—arranged for me to sneak away from the Institute."

Though her voice remained level and calm, he knew her three-month ordeal had been brutal. He didn't want to push too hard for details. "When you linked up with your contacts, why didn't you use them to get released? You have grounds to charge your ex-husband."

"Reality check—I don't dare challenge Hugh. He's a powerful man with high-powered attorneys. As for me? I'm easily dismissed as a divorced wife who was so depressed that I tried to commit suicide." Her mouth stretched into a straight, hard line. "I couldn't take the chance that I'd lose."

He didn't want to believe that the court system could be so easily corrupted, but he understood why she felt powerless. "When you're in the clear, I hope you write a tell-all book about your experience."

"Don't worry, I'll get my revenge when my ex-husband is in prison."

"Ex-husband, right? Did you sign the divorce papers?"

"I didn't have a choice. It was the only way he'd let me see the kids."

She spoke with an edgy determination that made him glad he wasn't the target of her rage. "What's our next step?"

"After we're settled at your cabin and I've got internet, I'll reopen my investigation. There's an important witness I'm tracking down. When my case is airtight, I'll present it to federal and state prosecutors who will charge Hugh and his criminal buddies."

"And you're sure this is solid evidence?"

"Explosive," she said with grim satisfaction. "In the meantime, I'll lay down my false trail in Las Vegas. There are tons of surveillance cameras to record my presence, and I met the owner of the Magic Lamp Casino, Caspar Khaled, when I visited last year. Caspar is kind of a gossip, and he'll be sure to report my visit to Hugh."

Blake didn't like the way this plan was shaping up. "Let me make sure I understand. You plan to contact this Khaled at the Magic Lamp."

"Me and the twins," she confirmed with some hesitation. "It's probably best if you don't accompany us. Can you find another way to meet us in Utah tomorrow morning?"

"There's a guy in Henderson who owes me a favor and could loan me a vehicle," he said. "I suppose you've already made travel arrangements for you and the twins."

"Do you remember the James Bond movie with the sexy female pilot?"

He paused to catch his breath. She'd tossed out a lot to consider—Caspar Khaled, the Magic Lamp and 007. Still, he remembered with a smile. "You're referring to the lady pilot, Pussy Galore."

"I know a real-life version. Her name is Emily Finnegan. She used to be a showgirl, but her real talent is poker. She won a helicopter and built her own fleet. I did a couple of articles on her business and the resulting publicity gave her a boost."

"Rags-to-riches story," he said.

"More like G-strings to g-force, if a chopper went that fast." She flashed a grin. "So? What do you think?"

"I'm not great at plotting like a criminal," he said, hoping to dash cold water on her enthusiasm for the adrenaline rush of dancing outside the law. "But I see flaws."

"Such as?"

"While you're in the Magic Lamp, Khaled has home-field advantage."

She nodded. "I'll move fast. And I'm counting on the element of surprise."

She wasn't being realistic about the danger of confronting a casino owner. Las Vegas might not be run by the mob anymore, but that didn't mean the city was totally family-friendly. "If you run into trouble at the casino, how will you keep the twins safe?"

"I've been worrying about that. We'll have to run. The kids are pretty darn speedy."

"Are they fast enough to outrun grown men who know their way around Vegas?"

Her brow furrowed. "This plan isn't going to work,

is it? But I don't have much choice. I can't very well leave the kids in the car."

"Things change," he pointed out. "You have me riding shotgun."

"True."

"I'm your backup."

"True, again."

He took his cell phone from his pocket and scrolled through his encyclopedic inventory of contacts until he found the listing for his buddy. "I'll call Harvey in Henderson. When we get to Las Vegas, you can head for the Magic Lamp, and I'll keep the twins out of harm's way."

She concentrated on the road when merging onto US 93, a highway that led to Lake Mead, Hoover Dam and Las Vegas. The increase in traffic was noticeable, even in the middle of the night. "We're more than halfway there," she said, "only an hour and forty-five minutes to go. We'll arrive between 1:30 and 2:00 a.m. My rendezvous with Emily is scheduled for 3:00 a.m."

"Call her and let her know I'm taking your place. Me and the twins will go to the airfield and meet up with Ms. Pussy Galore."

"A word of advice. Don't call her that to her face. She'll knock your block off."

"Thanks for the warning." He shrugged. "Are you okay with this change in plans?"

"I'm relieved. It's better not to put the kids in danger."

"Do you want me to come with you into the casino?"

Her jaw clenched. "I can handle myself."

IN AN ALLEY behind Fremont Street in the heart of old Las Vegas, which had been revamped with street performers, light shows, neon artwork and zip lines, Jordan tensed her grip on the car door handle and squeezed her eyes closed, mentally preparing herself before entering Caspar Khaled's casino. She blinked and checked her watch—2:13 a.m.

Their little troop had made two stops. Once in Henderson, where Harvey joined them with his SUV, and they formed a two-vehicle caravan for the balance of the drive. Their second stop was at a gas station where they shifted seating. The twins in their booster seats went into the SUV with Blake while Jordan rode in the passenger seat of the Prius with Harvey behind the wheel.

"Are you okay?" he asked.

"I think so." She had changed into a black outfit and a satin, neon green bomber jacket, which was designed to attract attention and then be easily discarded so she was wearing only black. In her jeans' pocket, she carried a switchblade that she hoped never to use. Her titanium baton that extended to twenty-six inches was holstered on her belt.

"Captain Delaney seems better," Harvey said. "I was worried about him."

She stared at Harvey's craggy profile, dominated by a nose that had obviously been broken more than once. Though his hair hung almost to his shoulders and his chin sported thick salt-and-pepper stubble, he carried himself like a marine. "Why were you worried about Blake?"

"His injuries after the IED explosion would have killed most men. Not the captain. When the docs told him he'd never walk again, he started training for a goddamned marathon."

Jordan knew nothing about his injuries. Every bit of her focus and energy had been directed at herself and her children with no room for anybody else. She and Blake had been riding in the Prius together for hours. He certainly could have said something. But she hadn't asked and felt deeply ashamed for not being more concerned. "He's recovered now, right?"

"How come you don't know?"

"I've been…out of touch…for the past three months."

"I get it." Even in the alley, reflected flashes from many colors of neon splashed across his face. "The captain don't like to talk about himself. Never whines, never complains. But that don't mean he ain't hurting. The top brass asked him to step back from field operations and take a more supervisory role. No way. Am I right? Captain Delaney ain't riding no desk."

Had he mentioned something about retirement? "Please tell me he's okay."

"Depends on your definition," Harvey said. "I will say this. You're good for him and so are the twins. I've never seen him so smiley."

As soon as she and Blake were together again, she'd get to the bottom of this explosion and possible retirement. For now, she needed to concentrate her energy on her mission. She inhaled, closed her eyes and visualized her goals: *Show my face to the cameras in the casino. Lay out a false trail for Khaled to pass on to Hugh.* Her eyelids lifted. It was 2:17 a.m. She opened the car door.

"Wait," Harvey said. "Where should I pick you up afterwards?"

"No need. I'll catch a cab."

"Just in case, I'm going to stick around. I'll be cruising on Fourth Street."

"Thanks, Harvey."

She blew him a kiss, closed the door and strolled down the alley to Fremont. On a Saturday night in October, the temperature hovered at a pleasant sixty-five degrees, and the streets hosted a mob of revelers, singing and dancing and having a good time. If she'd brought the twins, they would have been captivated by the churning overhead lights and blasting music from top rock stars. Alex would say they were trapped inside a video game while Cooper would, no doubt, find a wizarding comparison. The neon created an unnatural, mesmerizing atmosphere. Her contacts in Las Vegas had told her that she'd be picked up by surveillance cameras immediately, but she had trouble figuring out how anybody could find her in such a crowd.

When she slipped into the Magic Lamp Casino, Jordan took care to avoid metal detectors at the entrance. She meandered through slot machines toward the gaming tables. After being sequestered at the Institute for three months, she was overwhelmed by the casino's dazzling sensory overload. The Arabian Nights theme played out with cocktail waitresses in see-through harem pants and bejeweled bra tops wandering among the gamblers with free drinks. Belly dancers undulated on four circular stages. Shirtless young men, oiled and glistening, performed intricate sword dances that reminded her of kendo and the Filipino martial arts techniques she'd learned using her baton.

Amid the exotic background, the clanking of coins from machines paying out and mechanical voices beckoning gamblers to play combined in discordant harmony. She needed to get this unscheduled meeting with Khaled done so she could fly away with her boys.

She approached a well-dressed man in a shiny black suit and purple shirt with an open collar. His position at the center of several blackjack and poker tables made her think that he was the supervisor, the pit boss.

Tilting her head upward so she'd be readily visible on camera, she said, "Excuse me, I need to leave a message for Caspar Khaled."

Unsmiling, he replied, "Check at the front desk, miss."

The way she figured, her chances for escape were better on the casino floor where some of the gamblers crowded around looking for their next lucky break and others played with single-minded concentration, only occasionally glancing up at the jiggling belly dancers. Fixing her gaze on the pit boss, she spoke loudly. "It's okay to call him. I know him very well. Actually, my husband—" no need to mention that Hugh was an ex "—he's an associate of Mr. Khaled."

"I can't help you."

"My husband, Hugh Waltham, has political connections at the highest level. And he has business interests he shares with your boss." Though she didn't have enough evidence to make an accusation that would stick, she suspected Khaled's involvement with Hugh was all about money laundering. She gave the pit boss an exaggerated wink. "Business interests. You know what I mean?"

"A politician, huh?"

"I just want to leave a message." She fluttered her eyelashes in the direction she thought a surveillance camera might be recording. It would have been useful to have Blake with her. He could have pointed out the cameras. "Tell Caspar that Jordan Reese-Waltham is in town. I'm staying at the Flamingo. In a few days, I'll be at The Ritz-Carlton in San Francisco."

"What's this about?"

"A joint project." She shot him a huge, beaming smile. "Maybe you ought to write some of this down."

"What's your name again?"

"Jordan. Reese. Waltham."

He repeated it, then touched his ear, most likely listening to somebody through an earbud, and then grabbed her left arm above the elbow. Grabbed tight. His fingers dug into her flesh. "You need to stay with me."

His response surprised her. She'd expected to be mostly ignored, which was exactly how a pit boss usually acted. Best-case scenario: have her message passed on to Khaled, who would then contact Hugh and tell him she was headed to San Francisco. Worst outcome: Khaled wouldn't get the message, and she would have wasted her time.

She tried to twist away from him. "Let me go."

"Turns out that Mr. Khaled wants to see you."

Never had she thought the casino owner would be in his office at two in the morning, paying attention to camera feeds. She needed to get away from this thug and hustle out to the airfield.

As the pit boss dragged her through the crowd, she reached across her body with her right arm and unfastened her innocent-looking holster. About the size of her hand, the black case on her belt matched her outfit under the neon green jacket. She pulled out her baton. With a downward flick of her wrist, the titanium rod extended to twenty-six inches.

Her technique with the baton borrowed heavily from Japanese kendo and fencing, but the basics came from the Filipino martial arts that used rattan sticks. A calm came over her, boosting her confidence. *I can do this.* Twisting her body away from him, she whipped the baton against his elbow joint. With a gasp of pain, the pit boss released her. And she ran.

Weaving through the Saturday-night crowd, she sprinted toward the main exit, encountered another guy in a shiny suit and two of the bare-chested dancers with fierce expressions twisting their mouths, making them look like they wanted to munch on her arm for a post-midnight snack. *Retreat!* Jordan backpedaled and flew in the opposite direction.

Darting through the casino, bobbing and weaving, dodging around cocktail waitresses with trays of drinks, she found another way out. Three wide, carpeted stair-steps led to the street. At the top stood a huge man with a shaved head and heavy black eyebrows. He spread his arms, blocking her way. It was Caspar Khaled.

Chapter Five

When Jordan first met Khaled a couple of years ago, she'd recognized a glimmer of interest in his dark brown eyes, even though Hugh was standing right there. Neither she nor Khaled overtly flirted, but he'd kissed her hand instead of shaking it, opened doors for her and held her chair at a fabulous gourmet dinner in the Sultan's Cave. When speaking to her, his voice took on a husky tone that was suggestive in spite of his massive size. More than once, he'd asked her to try on a belly dancer's costume.

Not anymore. Like a soccer goalie, he was positioned on a landing at the top of three long stairsteps in front of the side-by-side, glass doors that opened onto Fremont Street. His dark brown guayabera shirt with strips of white embroidery down both sides stretched tightly over his chest. The short sleeves displayed muscular biceps and forearms. In spite of the modern clothes, he reminded her of an ogre—not a friendly cartoon monster but a ferocious creature known to devour babies. Going head-to-head with him would be foolish. She needed to distract, evade and escape.

"Happy to see you," she said as she tore off her

neon green jacket and wrapped it loosely around her left hand, leaving the right arm free to use the baton. "Hugh sends his regards."

"How would you know? Your husband divorced you."

"Let's get this straight. I divorced him." Maybe her ex was closer to Khaled than she'd thought. With the volume of cash that flowed in and out of his casino, there was a great opportunity for money laundering if the restrictions could be circumvented with the type of larceny that was Hugh's special talent.

He took a step toward her. "I just spoke to him on the phone."

Bad news for her. Had Hugh mentioned the kidnapping? He must have. That might be the reason Khaled and his men hadn't already knocked her unconscious. They needed her alert to take them to the twins.

From the corner of her eye, she saw the two barechested guys approaching with their patterned harem pants flapping around muscular thighs. Her expertise in the martial arts might not be enough to defeat three large men, but no one had ever accused her of lacking self-confidence. She wouldn't panic. She had to concentrate, needed to believe she could handle any obstacle. *I can get past them. I have to. For my sons.*

She surveyed her surroundings. To her amazement, the gamblers at the slots were too intent on their machines to notice the life-and-death struggle taking place. That indifference had to change. She counted on the crowd reaction to help her as she faced off with Tweedledum and Tweedledee. Jordan put on a show. Whirling and waving her neon jacket, she launched into a series of high kicks, some of which connected. She accompanied her action with loud shouts. "Hai. Hah. Ho."

Her gambit worked. The gamblers were watching. Some actually turned away from their slot machines. A couple of women shrieked and grabbed their purses.

Jordan dashed toward Khaled, saw that he was braced and ready for her attack and evaded his grasp while delivering a swift rap on his outstretched fingers with her baton. Instinctively, he pulled back.

The gamblers contributed shouts of their own. "Hai. Ho. Ho."

A pit boss stepped between her and the shirtless attackers. He made an announcement. "Nothing to worry about, folks. It's all part of the entertainment at the Magic Lamp."

She played along with his scenario with a couple of leg sweeps and more kicks accompanied by fierce poses with her baton. Like a star performer, she scampered back and forth across the stairs, then she took a bow. Finally, she twirled in front of Khaled and flung her jacket into his face. After a pivot, she dashed out the door onto Fremont Street.

The glittering chaos of neon lights and rock music suited her mood as she holstered her baton and dashed toward the hotels on the corner. From there, she could catch a taxi. Sensing the presence of cameras, she pulled up the hood on her fitted, nylon sweatshirt. Clad from head to toe in black, she felt as intangible as a shadow, darting swiftly through the crowd, which had thinned out a bit. Unfortunately, she wasn't invisible. Glancing over her shoulder, she glimpsed the pit bosses and shirtless men in pursuit.

At a western-themed hotel, she plunged into the underpass and spotted the line of taxis at the curb. Stopping to get inside one of these vehicles seemed like a sure way to get caught, and so she kept moving. Her thinking was disorganized. She hadn't planned for this turn of events, hadn't expected Khaled to react so aggressively. She still couldn't believe he'd immediately called Hugh. *Disaster!* Or maybe not. If nothing else, she had succeeded in establishing a false trail that would lead to San Francisco.

She ripped through the hotel's doors into the lobby, which featured an incongruous decor combining glittering chandeliers and ranch-style fences. Instead of harem girls and belly dancers, the cocktail waitresses dressed like cowgirls with red boots, vests and hats. The male employees looked like they were part of a rodeo, and all of them wore guns on their hips...toy guns, she hoped. To her left was the registration desk for the hotel, and beyond that she saw a long wooden bar like one in an old-time saloon. An arched entrance to the casino was to the right. She spun around and dashed up a staircase to the mezzanine. Hiding behind a huge pot holding a tall saguaro cactus, she could look down at the entrance. The gang from the Magic Lamp charged through the doors, conferred for a moment and then split up, probably to search for her.

If she'd had more time, Jordan would have ducked into a more secure hiding place and stayed there until the coast was clear. But her departure on Emily's chopper was scheduled for 3:00 a.m., and she didn't want to be late. Already, the time was 2:42.

When the Magic Lamp guys had dispersed, she

scampered down the staircase and out the door into the night. Turning on the speed, she headed for Fourth Street. Harvey said he'd cruise that area, and she hoped to find him. For a change, luck was with her. The Prius had just pulled up at a stoplight. Jordan threw herself into the passenger seat. "Go."

The former marine gunned the engine—a less than dramatic gesture in a hybrid. He cranked the steering wheel and swerved in an illegal right turn. Through the windshield, she spotted the shirtless thugs in harem pants. The Prius left them in the dust.

"I think we made it," she said.

"Just in case," he drawled, "I'm fixing to use evasive driving techniques." He accelerated and dodged through the late-night traffic like a Vegas native. "We damn sure don't want anybody hanging on our tail."

"Or following us to the airfield."

"Copy that." He left the main drag and zipped into a residential area, slowing his speed to match the few other cars on the road. "I don't mean to pry, but were those guys who looked like Aladdin's genies coming after you?"

"That's right." She could hardly believe she'd pulled off that escape.

"How did you kick genie ass?"

She showed him her baton and then collapsed it to fit back into the holster. "I have my ways."

"Damn, Jordan. You ain't playing around."

"Not when it comes to my kids."

Harvey drove with the assurance of a man who knew what he was doing. Nobody could follow this Prius. It helped that they weren't going to Harry Reid Interna-

tional Airport on Wayne Newton Boulevard but to a
private airfield where Emily kept her fleet. Also, Jordan had mentioned to the pit boss that she was staying
at the Flamingo, which should send them in the wrong
direction. This phase of her escape was over. At least,
she hoped it was.

After Harvey dropped her off, he would change the
license plates on the Prius and hand the vehicle off to
someone else who would take possession of the little
car while Harvey drove home to Henderson in his SUV.
Minutes clicked by on her wristwatch. Running late,
but it shouldn't be a problem. Her friend in Utah would
wait for her.

At 3:23 a.m., Harvey turned left onto a long, straight
road that led to the airfield on the outskirts of town
where several private companies and helicopter services
housed their aircraft. In the distance, beneath the flood-
lights, she spotted a blue-and-gold helicopter outside
a hangar. More importantly, she saw Blake, standing
nearly as tall as the chopper blades with the night wind
riffling through his short blond hair. His wide, muscular shoulders looked strong enough to carry whatever
she loaded upon him. Again, she felt a stab of guilt.
What gave her the right to burden him with her emotional baggage?

She hadn't bothered to find out what was going on
in his life. Harvey had said something about an IED
explosion and serious injuries. *I should back off.* It was
wrong to ask him to step into danger again.

WHEN BLAKE SPOTTED the Prius, he checked his watch.
At 3:27 a.m., she was nearly a half hour late. Jordan had

put him through twenty-seven minutes of raging anxiety. According to her damned plan, she was supposed to leave a message for Caspar Khaled at the Magic Lamp Casino and scamper out the door. *Yeah, right.* In what universe could she poke the bear and not expect a counterattack? She could have been shot or beaten or taken into custody.

No way should he have accepted her scheme. Blake knew what it meant to go into hostile situations. He was battle-trained. Not that his experience had helped in the most recent incident. When he got stuck in an IED explosion, he'd messed up. Big-time. And now, he doubted himself.

When she exited the Prius and strode across the tarmac toward him, he noticed a subtle difference in Jordan. Her curly brown hair had the same bounce. Her shoulders-back, athletic gait showed excellent physical conditioning. Her lips still curved in a confident grin, but her stormy blue eyes had taken on a new seriousness, and her fingers curled into fists. Whatever happened at the Magic Lamp had caused a shift in her attitude. He hoped this change would encourage her to consider the outcome of her actions before she—again—leaped with both feet into a churning sea of trouble.

When she was only a few feet away from him, he asked, "How did it go?"

She went up on tiptoe, wrapped her arms around his neck and molded her slender body to his. Her heart fluttered against his chest as she exhaled a long sigh. In a ragged whisper, she said, "I shouldn't have taken that chance. I almost blew the whole escape and got myself caught."

"You're not injured, are you?"

"No."

"And Khaled didn't follow you here?"

"No. Harvey's a great evasive driver."

"You bet I am." His buddy sauntered toward them. "She's right about that."

"In a way, my plan worked," she said. "Khaled already contacted Hugh and will undoubtedly tell him that I'm going to San Francisco. That's the false trail I want him to follow. But it could so easily have gone wrong. I didn't take the level of danger into account."

This was as much his fault as hers. He should have stopped her. *As if I could...* "You can't let your guard down now. Nor can I. We need to assume that Khaled is hot on our trail."

"And we have to get out of here pronto."

Keeping his arm slung around her shoulders, he leaned close and caught a whiff of her sweet jasmine and coconut shampoo. "In future, you might consider ways to adjust your style."

"You're right. I need to be more careful."

Ever since he'd known her, she'd been a risk-taker—a reporter who chose to be embedded with combat troops, an investigative journalist who tracked down a serial killer by posing as a prostitute, and now she was a single mother who had kidnapped her children and gone on the run. "Don't change too much, Jordan. I like you the way you are."

"But I ought to change…somewhat. And I intend to." She stared into his face, confronting him. "There's something else we have to talk about. But not in front of the kids."

As if on cue, the twins burst from the hangar, laughing and shouting as they ran toward her. She crouched and held out her arms to corral the rambunctious five-year-old boys. She held them close and kissed them a dozen times.

"You changed clothes," she said. More kisses.

"Didn't wanna run around in my jammies," Alex said.

"You're my big boys." More hugs and kisses.

"Cut it out, Mom." Alex pulled away. "Emily showed us the choppers. Awesome. I wanna be a pilot when I grow up."

"Me, too." Cooper snuggled in her arms as he pointed at the blue-and-gold helicopter. "That's an ECO-Star, made by Airbus. Oh, and the tail rotor is called a Fenestron which means fan-in-fin. Do you see it?"

Before she could reply, Alex interrupted. "It goes fast. That's all I want to know."

Blake hurried them along. "Are you boys ready for takeoff?"

The kids bounced up and down as they shouted a wildly enthusiastic assent. The time they'd spent sleeping in the car had apparently recharged their batteries. When Emily Finnegan—a stunning, six-foot-tall redhead—strode toward them, Harvey stepped closer to Blake and nudged his elbow. "I got to meet that woman."

The tone of his voice told Blake that his buddy wanted more than a handshake from the glamorous female pilot. Both were single. They shared a love of mechanics and speed. The minute he introduced them, sparks started to volley back and forth. Harvey moved fast, pulling a business card from the pocket of his weathered denim jacket. Emily responded in kind. This could be the start of a beautiful friendship.

Blake finished loading their duffel bags and the car seats into the cargo hold. He was impatient. Emily said the flight from Las Vegas to Fillmore, Utah, was about 250 air miles and, travelling at a speed of 125 to 150 miles per hour, would take roughly two hours. In Fillmore, they'd meet a former associate of Jordan's who had retired from a big-time career as a television news anchor to run a small weekly paper and spend all his free time on the nearby ski slopes. *Nice lifestyle.* Skiing and keeping track of local events might be something Blake would consider for his retirement.

During his tours of duty, he'd spent a lot of time in helicopters of all sizes and shapes. When it came to class and comfort, none compared with Emily's sleek, beautiful ECO-Star. Wraparound windows offered panoramic views. The leather seats were arranged with four, including the pilot's seat, in the front and four on a raised platform behind them. Though the boys wanted to sit in front, preferably on Emily's lap, she'd set up special elevated kid seats with safety harnesses in the rear where they still had outstanding views.

While Emily took her position in the pilot's seat and went through a series of preflight checks, Jordan climbed into the back with the boys and showed them how to wear the headsets. "These are voice activated," she said. "When Emily turns them on, we can hear every word you say, so don't be screaming into the microphone."

"Roger that," Alex said. "Emily said 'roger' means okay. And if it's not okay, you're supposed to say 'negative.'"

"And a helicopter is like a ship," Cooper said, not to be outdone when it came to new information. "That means we don't say left and right. It's 'port' and 'starboard.'"

"Starbucks," Alex said.

"Starboard. It means right."

While Jordan ran through the standard mom questions about potty breaks and drinking water and food, Blake turned to Emily. "Anything I can do to help?"

"Promise me that you won't let anything bad happen to Jordan and the boys." She dropped her voice so only he could hear. "The twins are precious cargo, and she's a good person."

Though he'd never spoken that promise, he'd already given his allegiance to this mission and to Jordan. From the moment he saw her and the twins in that garden shed, he had dedicated himself to bodyguard duty. Not that he was doing a great job as a protector. Why the hell hadn't he gone with her to the Magic Lamp? "I'll take care of them."

"Not an easy task. Jordan can be unrelenting and a little bit scary. Still, I'd do anything for her. And the twins? Oh my God, they're so smart and so active." Under her breath, she added, "I don't know how she keeps up with those little energy balls."

"Ditto."

She glanced toward the rear. "You guys get ready. I'm starting the engine."

Jordan made sure the twins were okay before she

moved to the front and settled into the seat between Blake and Emily. He had instinctively taken the outer seat, which was where he sat during most of his airborne military maneuvers when he needed to be the first out, directing his squad. Though he had braced himself for takeoff, the rumble of the rotors awakened unwanted memories of other flights, other missions. From the rear, the boys were screaming.

Blake clenched his jaw, fighting off a flashback. He hated the panicked, out-of-control feelings that came when he plunged into sensory recall. His nose twitched at the remembered stink of gunpowder. His ears rang with echoes of past explosions and the cries of the dying. He closed his eyes, blocking his visions of gunfire flashes, torn flesh and so damn much blood. His gut churned, and he tasted vomit in the back of his mouth. *Get a grip.* He told himself that they were taking off from Las Vegas in a chopper flown by a beautiful red-haired pilot. Forcing his eyelids open, he looked down and saw the shimmer of neon lights instead of jungle or desert.

Over the headset, Emily told them that she was turning off all the interior lights so they could have a better view. Though it was cool in the ECO-Star cabin, Blake felt sweat beading his hairline. The boys had ceased their screeching and babbled to each other about what they saw on the ground. They had no fear, none at all. Their voices on the headset were remarkably clear.

Emily informed them, "We're at an altitude of one thousand feet. I'll take a swing over the city, and then we're on our way to Utah."

Below lay Vegas. Glitter Gulch. On the strip, he saw

a replica of the Eiffel Tower, the skyline of Manhattan and a pyramid. Nothing to be scared of, and yet the thwap-thwap-thwap of the rotor and the vibration of the cabin stirred his visceral panic. His pulse thumped hard and fast. His chest was tight, and he couldn't breathe. For a moment, he felt the cabin closing in, suffocating him. *Can't pass out. Need to stay alert. Got to be strong.* And then, he felt Jordan's caress on his closed fist.

His fingers opened, and she gently cradled his hand. When he looked down at her, relief flowed through his veins. Her nearness soothed his tension and loosened the stranglehold of his flashback. Being here with her felt right. *We'll be okay.* He would protect her and the boys…or die trying.

Chapter Six

An hour and a half later, Blake studied Jordan's profile, trying to decide how she'd changed from when they'd first met. Her thick brown hair had been cut and styled since the days she'd been embedded with the troops and tamed her curls in a long braid. A slight evidence of aging showed in the laugh lines at the corners of her big blue eyes—those remarkable eyes. He saw an indefinable maturity in her expressions: she was slower to laugh and less likely to cry. He wished he could see more clearly. The only illumination inside the cabin came from the pilot's control panel, but he could see by the light of a full October moon—a hunter's moon.

Below the chopper, a vast western terrain unfolded. Though Zion and Bryce Canyon lacked the visual punch of Las Vegas neon, he preferred natural beauty. Early snow outlined the jagged peaks in the distance, reminding him of their final destination in the Colorado Rockies. These wonders would have impressed the two kids in the back, but they'd both nodded off to sleep.

Beside him, Jordan leaned toward Emily and asked, "Can you turn off the headsets for the boys so they can't hear us talking?"

"Sure thing. And I'll switch my headset to another channel so you and Blake can have a few minutes of privacy."

"Thanks." She turned toward him, and her eyes got even wider. "I never meant for things to turn out this way."

"Could be worse." He ran his fingers through his hair and inhaled the oily mechanical odor of the ECO-Star.

"I need to apologize for being so self-centered. During the whole time we've been on the run, I never asked about your life. I focused on my problems. I made it all about me."

He had a bad feeling about this conversation and hoped to head it off before she got started. "Apology accepted."

"Harvey told me you almost died."

Some veterans enjoyed sharing war stories. He wasn't one of them. Not clever or eloquent, Blake didn't have words to describe the pain, terror and grief he'd experienced. "Seriously, Jordan. Drop it."

"I can be a good listener," she said. "My skills as a reporter are kind of rusty, but they'll come back. You remember, don't you? Seven years ago, when we first met, do you remember how we talked?"

"You were interviewing me, wanted to write an article about the life of an average marine…as if there was such a thing. All marines are above-average." He gazed through the window at the panorama of canyons and mesas. Seven years ago. They'd been so young. So much had changed. "Things are different now."

"Tell me how you were injured."

"Don't know." He shrugged. "The incident is a blank."

"When did it happen?"

"Four months ago."

"Where were you?"

He recognized her tactic of poking inside his memories until she found something he recalled, like the color of his socks or what he had for breakfast. "You're not going to give up, are you?"

"I never do." The ECO-Star jostled, and her shiny brown hair bounced. "Now, let's start again. Where were you?"

"On a rutted, dirt road in a Land Rover with the top down. Should have taken an armored Humvee, but we expected this to be a quick trip."

He paused, allowing the memory to form. And he realized that the ride in the Rover to pick up beer and vodka for a party bore a horrible similarity to her jaunt into Las Vegas to pass a message to Khaled. The initial objective appeared to be clear and simple, but neither of them had considered the many things that could go wrong. In her case, the potential for disaster had been avoided. In his, catastrophe hit full force.

"The weather," she said. "What was the weather like?"

"The sky was clear, and the high desert sun glared down on us. I sat in the passenger seat, and there were three other guys. Two of them insisted that we leave right away so we could meet our contact person. I wanted to wait until one of the Humvees was free, but I relented. And I damn well paid the price."

"You can't blame yourself," she said.

"The hell I can't. I'm a captain. I was in charge. Taking care of those marines was my responsibility, and I let them down. When our Rover rolled over the IED, the device detonated. We had no warning, no time to prepare. One second, the road was all clear. The next, we were in the middle of a fiery explosion, tossed in the air like a kid's toys. Nobody died, but Lance Corporal Hodges lost his left leg above the knee. We were all injured, seriously injured."

Somehow, the touch of her hand conveyed empathy, and he believed her compassion was sincere. Jordan had been in combat and had experienced her own tragedies. Softly, she said, "What happened next?"

"I honestly don't remember." He winced. "They tell me that I put through a call for backup on my sat phone, which is kind of amazing because I can't believe the phone was still working. I pulled the other men clear. And I fired—left-handed because my right wrist was messed up—at an invisible enemy with my M16 and my handgun."

"And you don't remember any of this."

"Not a bit. The next thing I can recall was lying on an operating table with a bunch of medics in masks hanging over me, cutting off my clothes and waving scalpels. Stat-stat-stat. They kept saying it. I tried to talk, to ask about the other marines, but I couldn't make a peep. I looked down at my body and saw blood and guts—deep lacerations, contusions and abrasions. Hell, I was a mess."

She stroked his cheek, then gently turned his face toward her. Her steady gaze reassured him and made him feel that everything was going to be all right, even though he knew nothing would ever be the same. She asked, "Did you have broken bones?"

"A couple of ribs and my right wrist." He pulled

down his sleeve to hide the scars. "I'll probably never regain full range of motion. I'm learning how to shoot with my left hand."

"Any other permanent injuries?"

"I lost a piece of my right lung and one of my kidneys. I have muscle and nerve damage in both legs. Physical therapy is helping, but I might never return to peak condition."

And that was the problem. According to the doctors, he wasn't fit for full-time duty in a combat zone. Blake wished he could object to their opinion, but he knew they were correct. His marksmanship had been compromised, he couldn't run at top speed and his stamina was shot to hell. His formerly excellent skills in martial arts were no longer swift and sure. Jordan could probably kick his ass in kendo and karate. *How pathetic is that!* He'd been her first teacher—her first sensei.

She asked, "What comes next for you?"

Though he could continue his career, Blake would probably be assigned to desk work, maybe at the Pentagon or training recruits at Parris Island. That vision of the future felt as bleak and empty as the night sky that wrapped around the chopper. After he'd gotten out of the hospital and done the basic rehab, he had taken this time off to map his future. "I might retire."

She gasped, and he considered it a testament to the high quality of the ECO-Star headset that he could hear that sharp intake of breath. He had surprised her. Ever since they'd known each other and fallen in love, their careers had gotten in the way of their relationship. When they met, she was destined for great things as a journalist, and she wouldn't give up her ambitions to become a military wife. Likewise, he loved his work and lived for every day on active duty as a marine.

She leaned against him. The steady thump of the rotors provided a harsh background sound. "I know how much your work means to you," she said. "What are you going to do?"

"I'm not sure about tomorrow, but right now I'm going to make sure you and the twins are safe. That's my mission."

"I like that." After caressing the line of his jaw, she pulled him toward her and kissed his cheek. "I like it a lot."

"Don't be so sure," he said. No way would he have a repeat of this evening's mad dash into Vegas. "If I'm going to be responsible for you, I've got to be in charge. That means you either follow my instructions or come up with a damn good reason why you can't."

Her eyebrows pulled into a scowl. "I'm not good at taking orders."

But she'd already admitted her mistake—facing off with Khaled had been dangerous. "Let me remind you that your initial plan in Vegas included taking the twins into the casino with you. I convinced you that putting the kids in jeopardy wasn't a good idea."

"But I wasn't hard to convince." She stood up for herself, which was what he'd expected her to do. Jordan wasn't the type of woman who gave up control. "I won't be docile and utterly obedient, but I'm always willing to listen to reason."

"We share the same goal," he said. "Staying safe, which means minimal risk."

"The secondary goal is uncovering enough evidence

to get Hugh charged with bribery, extortion, wire fraud, embezzlement and maybe even murder."

Murder? She hadn't mentioned homicide before. "When we get to the cabin, we'll organize our objectives and decide how to proceed. Until then, no more impulsive actions."

"Agreed." She shook his hand.

"What's this about murder?"

"A long story." She turned her head and peered through the windshield at the endless depth of darkness beyond the stars and the moon.

He reached across her body, held her chin and turned her head toward him. Earlier she'd given him a peck on the cheek, a small intimacy that left him wanting more. He answered with a firm kiss on her full, pliant lips. She tasted as sweet as cherries, and her fragrance eclipsed the mechanical smell of the helicopter. She transported him.

He leaned back in the leather seat and closed his eyes.

AFTER JORDAN GAVE Emily the signal that she and Blake had finished their private conversation and the communication channel in the headset could be opened, she turned her head to stare at the man sleeping beside her. His kiss still tingled. She glided her tongue across her lips and felt the unquenchable spark of passion they'd shared seven years ago. If she hadn't gotten pregnant with the twins, she wouldn't have married Hugh and would surely have returned to Blake. Or maybe not. Jordan had been an ambitious young woman who wanted to make her mark in the world.

Blake's chest rose and fell as his breathing deepened. *Impossible!* After that kiss, she couldn't believe he was falling asleep while her hormones performed a wild, sensual *lambada*, the forbidden dance.

She spoke into the headset. "So, Emily, how much longer?"

"About forty-five minutes." The redheaded pilot gave her a friendly grin. "I have some good news."

"Let me have it. I could use something cheerful."

"I just talked to my partner at the airfield hangar, and he told me that nobody has been asking around about late-night flights. Nobody's been looking for me." She gave a nod. "I think you're safe, at least for the moment. You managed to sneak away from Las Vegas without anybody knowing where you're headed."

Jordan exhaled audibly, letting some of her tension ease. "Very good news, indeed. Khaled has had time to figure out that I'm not registered at the Flamingo. He's probably reported to Hugh."

"Just in case," Emily said, "I plan to leave Utah as soon as I drop you off and hurry home. Nobody knows I was out tonight except my partner, and I trust him."

"I can't thank you enough for helping us."

"Stop it," Emily said. "Without you and your articles, I never would have established my own business. The only thanks I want is an invite to your wedding."

"Whoa there, lady. I'm not looking to get married. I tried it once, and I'm not very good at it."

"Don't let one loser dictate your whole life. You and Blake are sheer perfection." She paused. "With emphasis on the sheer. That happens to be the title of the last show I appeared in."

"And I'll bet you brought the perfection."

"Whatever." She shrugged. "In the meantime, you ought to follow Blake's example and take a nap. You've got a long day of driving tomorrow, going from Fillmore to wherever you're headed in Colorado."

Jordan had purposely avoided mentioning their final destination. The fewer people who knew, the better. "You're right. I need sleep."

She closed her eyes, trying to clear her mind and slide into slumber. Immediately, she ran into obstacles. There were a dozen things to do, starting with a call to Abigail to make sure she was safe. In Fillmore, her old friend and mentor, Michael Hornsby, would provide them with a vehicle, and she had another task for him.

Her mind wouldn't settle. Details swirled in dizzying array. Through the headset, she heard the twins mumble in their sleep and twisted around to see them. They appeared to be fine, doing well. But how long would their complacent mood last? She needed to have a long talk with each of them about leaving their father and starting a new life. How would she explain her investigation? Though she was compiling evidence against Hugh, the children couldn't be expected to understand. If she'd been given a choice, she might have preferred to step back and let her ex-husband get away with his criminal schemes. *No way. Not a chance.* Her last confrontation with Hugh showed her that he was capable of terrible retribution. His hired thug had nearly killed her.

She fidgeted in the leather seat, shifted her weight from one side to the other and tangled her fingers in a knot. "Can't sleep."

"Nervous?" Emily asked.

"A little bit." If she were totally honest, her tension ran deeper than a case of nerves. Jordan was scared to death of what she was attempting and what might be lurking around the corner. Her fear of impending events kept slapping her awake. "I can't settle down. Tell me about your business. Maybe I can do another article about you and your choppers."

Emily talked, and Jordan listened, making mental notes for later when she could put together a story about her friend's success. Jordan had worried that she'd lost her journalistic skills, but the ability to focus and ask the right questions was deeply ingrained. And she needed the distraction. Thinking of somebody else's story allowed her to forget her own woes.

Beyond the windows, the night began to thin. Sunrise would bring a new set of challenges. Fresh adventures. More danger. Hugh would never let her get away with this. Her ruse in Las Vegas wouldn't fool him for long. The threat of his vengeance stalked through the dark caverns of her mind, coming ever closer, inescapable.

Without opening his eyes, Blake took her hand. Though she didn't want to admit it, she needed his protection.

Chapter Seven

The city of Fillmore in Millard County, Utah, honored the thirteenth US President, Millard Fillmore, who happened to be in office during the early 1850s when the county was founded by the territorial legislature. For a brief time, Fillmore had been the capitol of Utah Territory. As far as Jordan could tell, the city never regained its past glory and had become a pleasant, little place with a decent municipal airport.

At 6:55 a.m. Utah time, the ECO-Star landed outside a hangar at the far edge of the runways, and the rotors stopped twirling. Jordan took off her headset, and for a moment, reveled in the echoes of silence. She looked over her shoulder into the rear row of seats. "Are you kids okay?"

They pulled off the headsets, wriggled against their safety harnesses and started chattering. They both needed to go to the bathroom, and they were hungry, really hungry.

"So am I," she said.

"Breakfast sounds good." Blake reached into the back to release the twins from the seat belts. "I'm thinking of waffles."

"I want a pumpkin latte," Alex said.

"Coffee?" Jordan questioned.

"Dad said it was okay."

"Yeah," Cooper chimed in. "Dad lets us have coffee all the time."

She tamped down her irritation. Feeding caffeine to five-year-old kids was wrong for so many reasons, but now wasn't the time to complain about her ex-husband's lousy parenting skills. She climbed out of the cabin and helped the kids down to the tarmac. "Your choices are water, juice, milk or cocoa."

Peering through the dawn, she spotted Michael Hornsby leaning against the prefab wall of the hangar beside the huge, open doors. A tall, lean man with thick silver hair combed straight back from his tanned forehead, Hornsby had been her mentor from the time she snagged her first paying job as a journalist until she took an extended leave after giving birth. She trusted him implicitly and didn't like the way he was scowling. His deep-set eyes, his brows and even his long nose seemed to express disapproval. Something was wrong.

She approached him cautiously. Her hands rested on her kids' shoulders, and she brought them to a halt in front of the retired news anchor. "Alex and Cooper, you've met this gentleman before, but you were babies and too young to remember. This is Mr. Hornsby, the man who taught me almost everything I know."

As they'd been trained, the twins shook hands with her mentor and politely said, "Pleased to meet you, sir."

Hornsby's scowl evaporated like dew on a sunny morning. The adorable boys with their tousled brown hair and big, blue eyes had that effect on people. Hornsby dug into the pockets of his khaki trousers and pulled out a handful of change, which he distributed between the kids. "Inside the hangar," he said, "there's a vending machine with snacks. If it's okay with your mom, go for it."

"No chocolate." She tried to rein in the temptations. "Only one snack."

As they took off toward the machine, Blake stepped forward and introduced himself. "Jordan has told me a lot about you."

"She met you when she was embedded with the troops, correct?"

"Yes, sir."

"I was a newspaper editor back then. What did you think about the way she portrayed you in her article?"

"I speak for every marine in my platoon when I say that she did an excellent job. She understood us in a way that few civilians could."

While they discussed combat news coverage, she could tell that Blake and Hornsby liked and respected each other—a mutual appreciation that pleased her. Happiness bubbled up inside. These two men ranked high among the most important people in her life.

"I'm glad you're with her," Hornsby said to Blake, "because she's going to need all the help she can get. I had a call on my private cell phone about an hour ago from her ex-husband. He told me that Jordan suffered a nervous breakdown, and he had to find her before she injured herself or anyone else."

Her moment of joy popped like a bouquet of balloons. "You didn't believe him, did you?"

"Hell, no."

"He must have gotten your phone number from an old address book or my computer contacts."

"He has your computer?" Hornsby questioned.

She nodded. When Hugh and Gorilla Gruber attacked her and sent her off to the Institute, he stole her laptop. Though her files were encrypted, she suspected that he'd gained access and knew about some of her research into his criminal activities. Fortunately, she'd been smart enough to bury the more sensitive details in a tiny laptop that she tucked away in a safe-deposit box. "I'm sorry to drag you into this mess."

"Not a problem for me, but for you. He's trying to track you down." Hornsby glanced toward Blake. "If he has her contacts, he's probably trying to reach you as well."

Jordan asked, "What did you say to him?"

"Hey, I'm an old reporter. I know how to say 'no comment' in ways that won't arouse suspicion. And I might have played the old geezer card."

"What's that?" Blake asked.

"Pretended to be an old grouch which, of course, I'm not. I grumbled in a semi-coherent manner, causing that smug son of a gun to think I'm too ancient to know what's happening, certainly not sharp enough to aid Jordan in her escape. His call came through at a little after four in the morning. So the 'old geezer' persona was a fairly accurate portrayal of how I was feeling."

She wrapped her arms around him and squeezed. "I knew you'd have my back."

"And I got you a nifty Chevy SUV that I'll need to have returned in a few weeks." He hugged her back.

"Now, I want to talk to the twins and to meet your beautiful redheaded pilot."

"We can't stop for long," she said.

"You've got to eat," he said. "And I know a diner where the waffles are fluffy and the coffee is hot."

"No coffee for the kids," she said.

"Who'd do a damn fool thing like giving them caffeine? Seems to me those boys are plenty wide awake without artificial stimulation."

She linked her arm through his. "There's something else I need to talk to you about."

"I know that tone," Hornsby said. "You have a piece you're working on."

"That's it," she said. "A project."

And this project represented the most important work she'd ever done as an investigative reporter. The stakes couldn't be higher. Her survival and the future of her children depended on the evidence she compiled. If there had been more time, she wouldn't have asked Hornsby to help. The potential for danger was very real.

She glanced over her shoulder and saw Blake. He looked up from the screen on his phone and made eye contact. It occurred to her that she ought to talk over her plan with him before charging forward. Hadn't she just promised to let him take the lead? But discussion seemed unnatural. Jordan didn't usually work with a partner. Her reporting had always been solo. Clearly, that had to change. Before confiding in Hornsby, she'd talk to Blake.

When the twins rejoined them, showing off their choices for one-snack-each, Jordan took advantage of the interruption. "I'm sure Mr. Hornsby would like to hear about your experiences on the helicopter."

"I always enjoy a good story," her mentor said, showing the same attention and encouragement to her sons that he'd given to her when she was a bright-eyed cub reporter. "Did that pretty lady pilot let you fly it?"

"She should have," Alex said with unshakable confidence.

"You're such a dope." Cooper got in a dig.

"Why? Because I want to fly choppers instead of wizard brooms?"

Cooper looked up at Hornsby. "Do you believe in wizards?"

"Some of my best friends are magical. Like your mother."

Cooper took his hand and pulled him toward a picnic table outside the hangar while Alex tore open the wrapper on his granola bar. Fondly, she watched them, wondering if Cooper—who loved to make up stories—would grow up to be a reporter. Or maybe Alex. He certainly had the curiosity and bravado. She rubbed at her eyes, wishing she'd managed to take a nap on the chopper. An hour and a half of shut-eye would have made a difference.

Blake stepped up beside her. "That project you wanted to talk to Hornsby about—does it have to do with your investigation into your ex?"

"Yes, and it's not exactly risk-free."

"Tell me more."

Sharing information with him felt right. She reached into her pocket and took out a key chain with two keys and a small, rotund plastic penguin. "His name is Tux, and he's a flash drive."

"Wow," he said with a straight face. "You're just like the CIA."

"All the evidence I've gathered on Hugh is recorded here."

"Not on the computer he swiped?"

"I hid the sensitive files, including names of possible witnesses, on a tiny computer that I kept in a safe-deposit box. That info is triple-encrypted. As soon as I gained access to a computer while I was in the Institute, I contacted a computer genius who remotely retrieved my data."

"Smart." His compliment rang true.

As an investigative reporter, she'd developed great resources in the computer world. Hackers, programmers and cyberspies were among her best buddies. "And I have a copy of Tux hidden with my stuff."

"Another penguin?"

"A fat flamingo," she said with a grin.

"How do these strange birds connect to Hornsby?"

Though it went against her natural instincts, she'd agreed to share her plans with him and intended to fulfill her part of the bargain. "I want to give Tux to Hornsby for safekeeping in case anything happens to me. Also, I'll find a way to communicate more details to him as I collect them."

Blake nodded. "He's your backup, somebody you trust to go after Hugh if, for some reason, you can't."

"Exactly." When he framed her plan in those terms, it seemed even more dangerous.

"Does he know what to do with the information?"

A fair question. If this had been a matter of writing an exposé, she'd trust Hornsby to have the best resources. But her case was geared toward providing federal prosecutors with the data they needed to put Hugh out of the crime business and land him in prison. "I included the names of my contacts in Tux. Here's my problem: I don't want to put Hornsby in jeopardy. Is it fair to ask him to do this?"

"He's a perceptive guy," Blake said. "Hornsby knows how much risk he can handle. Explain what you need, including the part about suspecting Hugh of complicity in a murder, and leave the final decision up to him."

"Is that an order, Captain?"

"More like a suggestion." The corner of his mouth lifted in a half grin. "Thanks for telling me your plan."

She gave a satisfied nod. She still wasn't thrilled about the need for backup, but her arrangement with Blake seemed to be working. "Do we have time for breakfast?"

"I'd like to get on the road as soon as possible." He held up his cell phone. "While you drive, I have some text messages to return."

"You shouldn't use your phone," she said. "The location can be traced, can't it?"

"I disabled tracking before we left Arizona." He glared at the phone in his hand. "I still don't completely trust this thing. You have other untraceable burner phones, right?"

"Only four are left, not including this one, which is my superphone, prepped and programmed by my computer genius." She took it from her pocket. "This innocent-looking device is encrypted and bounces the signal through hundreds of locations. You want to talk CIA? This is the real deal. Give me your phone, and I'll transfer your contacts onto this one."

He handed the cell phone over. "You like this spy stuff."

"I'm glad I can use it," she said, as she quickly made the transfer and gave his phone back. "I hate that spy stuff is necessary."

"Good answer." He dropped his cell phone to the smooth concrete floor in the hangar and ground the heel of his boot into the screen. "Now it's just plastic."

"A little violent but effective." She tapped the edges of her encrypted, untraceable cell phone. "You can use this one after I finish my call to Abigail."

"What are you going to tell her?"

"As little as possible. If she has information for me, that's great. But I'm going to encourage her to step away. She thinks this is a game—doesn't realize how dangerous Hugh and Gruber can be."

While Blake went toward the picnic table to join Hornsby and the twins, she put through her call. At 7:33 a.m. in Utah, it was an hour earlier in Flagstaff, not too early. Abigail, a fitness nut, was usually up at dawn's first light, jogging on the mountainous trails near her house.

The cell phone rang six times, seven times... Was she still asleep? Three more rings. Jordan glanced at the specially encrypted phone. Her name wouldn't show on caller ID because the phone was untraceable, but she'd called twice before, and her friend had answered without hesitation. *Come on, Abigail, pick up.*

The voice that answered was a stranger. "This is Abigail Preston's phone."

"May I speak to her?"

"Who is this?"

That authoritative tone didn't belong to an assistant or someone who worked in Abigail's house. Jordan feared that something had happened, something terrible. "What's going on? Let me talk to Abigail. Who is this?"

"Officer Rita McNally, Flagstaff PD."

Jordan turned away so the kids, Blake and Hornsby couldn't see her horrified expression. Her pulse stopped. She felt the blood drain from her face. *No, this can't be happening.* She choked out the words. "I don't understand."

"I need your name, ma'am."

Jordan gasped and shook herself. Now was not the time to freeze up. "Was Abigail hurt?"

"There was an accident. Her car went off the road."

"Is she all right? Which hospital has she been taken to?"

"I'm sorry, there's nothing more I can say."

"I need to know," she said hoarsely. "Please, tell me."

"You'll have to call her husband."

Like hell she would. Stanley Preston worked with her ex-husband and idolized him. It might be possible that Stanley played a part in Abigail's supposed accident. Surely not. They appeared to be one of the happiest couples Jordan knew. But appearances could be deceptive. At one time, she'd thought herself in love with Hugh.

"Ma'am," the officer said. "Tell me your name."

Jordan disconnected the call. Her reporter's instincts

told her that Abigail was dead. Otherwise, the officer would have given her a hospital. But she wasn't certain. She needed verification. Her computer genius, Spike Mauritius, could tap into the internal documents and communications of the Flagstaff PD. No matter how much she dreaded the truth, Jordan had to find out, had to dig deeper.

There were only two things she knew for sure. Whatever had happened to Abigail wasn't an accident. And she—Jordan Reese-Waltham—was to blame.

Chapter Eight

On the road again, Blake sprawled in the passenger seat of the Chevy Suburban, enjoying the extra legroom. Both the Prius and the helo had been okay, but the seating in this wide SUV gave him the room to spread out—pure luxury. He kept a watchful eye on Jordan as she drove north on the highway. She hadn't slept at all last night, but exhaustion took second place to the grief, horror and guilt that consumed her. The muscles in her jaw were tensed. Her lips stretched in a taut, straight line. As sunlight slanted across the horizon, she turned off the headlights and slipped on a pair of sunglasses that didn't cover the dark smudges below her eyes.

After she'd told him in a few terse sentences about Abigail's "accident," she'd put on a determinedly upbeat expression that he recognized as her mom mask. No matter what else was happening, even if the sky was falling, she wouldn't allow her emotions to show because she had to protect the kids, didn't want to scare them.

Though he wasn't buying her stoic attitude for one hot minute and knew she was hurting, he admired her ability to compartmentalize her feelings, a skill he often practiced when planning a mission or facing the negative results of failure. After the incident with the IED when the docs told him that he might never walk again, he'd gritted his teeth and tripled his time in physical therapy. Instead of raging at the fates or breaking down in tears, he'd concentrated on what was possible. More exercise would improve his odds of recovery. He didn't allow himself to dwell on the likelihood of being assigned to a desk job. Instead, he spent his time considering different future possibilities…maybe a life that included Jordan. He always tried to present a strong front to the rest of the world.

The shrink had told him that compartmentalizing led to increased stress and PTSD. He'd advised Blake to face his traumas rather than avoiding them, because they wouldn't go away. How long could he ignore the pain? Lock away the anger about muscles and nerves that didn't work? Yeah, the shrink might be right. Someday, Blake might unlatch the compartment and allow misery to pour over him. But not today.

Chatter from the twins in the back seat alerted him to the probability that they sensed something was wrong. Like him, the boys didn't buy their mother's fierce calm. Blake needed to deal with them. If the kiddos didn't settle down, this six-to-eight-hour cross-country leg of their journey would feel like an eternity.

In a low voice, he spoke to Mama Bear. "The cubs need feeding. We can grab breakfast at a drive-through."

Though he hadn't seemed to be paying attention, Alex picked up on what Blake said. "Yeah, Mom. We're starving."

"I want a muffin," Cooper said. "Two muffins and bacon."

"No eating in the car," Jordan said automatically. "You know the rules."

"And no junk food," Cooper said.

"No fair." Alex pouted. "We gotta eat something."

"When we get to Salina, we'll stop for breakfast," she said. "Keep watching the road signs. You can count down the miles."

"Salina is still in Utah," Blake said, "but that's where we hook into eastbound I-70. After that, our route couldn't be simpler."

He'd driven this way many times before, sticking to I-70 past Grand Junction and through the Rockies to his cabin at Ice Mountain. If the worst happened and Hugh got wind of their destination, Blake knew how to elude anyone who tried to follow.

Behind him, he heard the inevitable questions from the twins.

"Are we there yet?" Alex asked. "How much longer?"

"How many miles?" Cooper piled on.

Blake made approximate calculations from the last mileage sign for Salina. "We've got thirty-three minutes to go."

There was a chorus of groans and complaints and statements about how they'd pass out from starvation before they got to Salina. Blake figured that the twins weren't much different from newbie recruits. The best way to get them to cooperate was to distract them. With recruits, he could wave a shiny beer can in front of their eyes. And with the five-year-old boys... Blake turned on the screens for the rear-seat entertainment centers and handed the kids the attached headphones.

"Cartoons," Cooper cheered.

"Awesome," his brother joined in.

The sound accompanying the screen images went silent when the headphones were activated. So did the twins. Blake glanced at Jordan and said, "I'm sure you'd rather not have them glued to the cartoon channel, but I need a break."

"Not a problem," she said. "Do you think they can hear us talking?"

He glanced into the rear and saw matching rapt expressions on the boys' faces as they stared at a cartoon Dalmatian in a firefighter's helmet. He tested their ability to hear by saying in a normal voice, "Did I ever tell you about how I can fly? My favorite food is raw squid."

No reaction from the peanut gallery. He turned to Jordan and said, "They won't overhear a word we say."

"About Abigail." In spite of his reassurance, her tone was soft. Her voice trembled with worry. "Her house is high in the Peaks outside Flagstaff, and those roads are relatively narrow with some hairpin turns. It's conceivable that she had an accident after the fundraiser."

"Conceivable," he echoed.

"But she drove that route every single day."

He wanted real information, facts. "When will you hear back from your computer genius?"

"He didn't give me a specific time."

"Are you ever going to tell me his name?"

"He uses several different handles," she said. "The guy is a legendary hacker with contacts at the highest and the lowest levels. He practically lives on the dark web, and he doesn't like for people to know him. I call him Spike."

No surprise that she'd buddied up to a scary cyberge-nius. Sweet, little Jordan with her shining brown curls and innocent blue eyes had a talent for attracting and taming complex people. "We should wait for Spike to get back to us with the facts from the Flagstaff PD. In the meantime, I think it's smart to assume the worst and plan from there."

"So we assume that…" Her voice caught in her throat and dropped to a whisper. "We've got to assume she's dead."

"Murdered by your ex-husband and his security chief," Blake said. "Let's also assume they questioned her. Before her so-called accident, how much did she tell them? How much did she know?"

A tear leaked from the corner of Jordan's eye, but she kept her attention on the road. "Every time I talked to her, I told her we weren't playing a game. Damn it, I warned her to be careful. Since I didn't want her to be forced to lie, I never mentioned the route I planned to take or that our destination was Ice Mountain."

"Before last night, did you talk to her about the time we spent together in Colorado?"

"I don't think so. The only time we talked about you was when you came to visit and meet the boys who were two-year-old terrorists in diapers."

That long weekend in Flagstaff nearly broke his heart. Jordan glowed with happiness, and the kids looked just like her. Her husband had been out of town, and Blake had desperately wanted to step into that role. "It's when I met Abigail, and she insisted on giving me her phone number."

"You talked to her yesterday," she said, "when you

were looking for me. Did you say anything incriminating?"

"I didn't know squat. Until I met you in the garden shed, I had no idea we'd be going on the run. When I talked on the phone to Abigail, I didn't have a damn thing to tell her." He shrugged. "I might have whined a little bit."

She gave a snort and wiped away her tear. "You're cute when you whine."

"No man ever needs to hear that they're cute."

"Well, you are. With your dimples and crinkled forehead."

"Please. Stop."

She exhaled in a gush, and her mouth relaxed into something resembling a smile as she glanced over her shoulder into the rear seats. "I'm glad they're quiet, but I'm not going to let them watch cartoons all day."

He stayed focused on the current problem. "Assume she was questioned. You didn't tell her anything. And I didn't, either. Earlier last night, I bumped into Gruber on the grounds behind the mansion but didn't tell him anything. I don't think we have a problem."

"She was murdered. I call that a big problem." Her brief smile was gone, and her mood darkened. "It's my fault."

From his years in combat, Blake knew that blaming yourself for the loss of someone else, especially in combat, didn't make logical sense. The only person responsible was the one who pulled the trigger. But he understood how Jordan felt. Losing a friend was never easy.

He reached across the center console and stroked her

arm while the Suburban rushed along the two-lane, divided highway leading to Salina. The dawn light spread across the high plains where the foothills had turned a dusty autumn brown and the Valley Mountains were iced with new snow. Weather predictions for the West indicated an early winter, and he hoped the heavy snow would hold off until Jordan finished her investigation into her ex-husband.

After giving her arm a final squeeze, he said, "I should use this quiet time to return messages from two people Hugh contacted to get information about me."

"How would he know these people?"

"Wouldn't take much to track them down. I noticed the messages before I destroyed my phone."

"Make your calls." She gave a knowing nod. "It's always wise to take care of business while the kids are absorbed by something else."

Using her super-encrypted phone, he texted his commanding officer and the clinical supervisor at Walter Reed to let them know he'd gotten their messages and his phone was out of order. Without mentioning his location, he indicated that he'd be on vacation and would stay in touch before he was expected to return to duty next month. He had one more call to return. It came from the man himself: Hugh Waltham.

When they reached Salina, Jordan drove into the parking lot for a diner beside a corner lot with a couple of scrubby pine trees and a small playground. As soon as they were out of the car, the twins launched themselves onto the monkey bars. In contrast, Jordan moved slowly, as though her sneakers were made of concrete. She took a seat on the bench beside a picnic table to watch the kids while Blake went inside and ordered breakfast to go, including a giant coffee for himself and a decaf for Jordan. Like it or not, the woman needed to sleep.

He brought the take-out bags of muffins, egg-and-sausage sandwiches, Tater Tots and orange juice to the playground and set them on the picnic table that Jordan had swept clean of fallen leaves. Though the air held a chill, the morning sunlight beamed down on the playground, warming their little group. While the twins tore into their food like starving critters, Jordan lifted her sunglasses and gazed across the picnic table at him. Though she hadn't recovered her equilibrium after the tragedy of losing her friend, her eyes reflected openness and trust as she shared her grief. Being a part of this little family felt special. He'd do anything to protect them.

And that included making a phone call to Hugh. Taking her super-encrypted phone, he left the table. "I'll be back. I need to put through one more call."

He strolled down the sidewalk in the small town, passing unlit storefronts. It was still too early for most places to open. The gas station on the corner showed signs of activity, and the lights were on in the pharmacy. But the only other signs of life centered on the diner.

Blake stared at the screen on the phone. Before he punched in Hugh's number, he reminded himself of the need for control. This callback was supposed to be a simple courtesy, but his real goals were twofold. First, he hoped to distance himself from Jordan so Hugh wouldn't follow clues that pointed toward him. Second, he wanted to learn how much Hugh had figured out about Jordan's escape.

Though he'd never met Jordan's ex-husband, Blake recognized his voice from Hugh's appearances on news shows. He introduced himself. "This is Captain Blake Delaney. I'm returning your call."

"You're the marine," Hugh said.

"Yes."

"What took you so long to call back?"

"My phone is broken."

"You and I seem to be missing connections," Hugh said. "My security chief, Ray Gruber, met you on the grounds outside my house last night, but I didn't see you inside."

"I changed my mind about attending a party."

"Any particular reason?"

"I'm not accustomed to galas. String quartets, canapés and ball gowns scare me more than fire fights." *Not entirely a lie.* "I walked for a while, called a car service and went back to my motel."

Blake felt like he was talking too much. He ran his thumb across his lips in a reminder to himself to let Hugh speak and spill the beans.

"You know my ex-wife," Hugh said. "Did you come to the fundraiser to see her?"

"I hoped to."

"I see." His tone held a combination of disgust and disbelief. "Did you find her?"

"No."

A complicated lie about trying to visit Jordan at the Institute occurred to him, but he said nothing. From the television news shows, he recalled an image of Hugh. Not just another talking head, the political consultant from Arizona was younger and better-looking than most, with blond hair, tanned cheeks and swampy green eyes. His features balanced in near-perfect symmetry, and his extremely white teeth glistened like a shark's.

Hugh cleared his throat and asked, "Did you know Abigail Preston?"

His use of the past tense was chilling. "I met her a few years ago."

"And you spoke to her recently."

"She told me about the fundraiser and suggested that Jordan would be there to show her support for your campaign. I wanted to see her."

"Hah! Abigail wouldn't tell you that." This time, Hugh didn't bother to camouflage his disdain. "My ex-wife doesn't support me. She holds me back, drags me down."

Blake gritted his rear molars so hard that his jaw hurt. At this point in their conversation, he should probably make some comment to show he was on Hugh's side and considered Jordan a difficult woman. But he couldn't do it, not even in jest. "Why did you call me?"

"I know you were in love with her. Having you turn up on my doorstep on the same night that she staged an escape from the Institute was too great a coincidence to ignore."

He hadn't mentioned the kidnapping—an odd omission. "Escaped? You make it sound like she was being held prisoner."

"Part of her delusion," Hugh said, smoothly covering the real story. "She's deranged, a very sick woman."

His practiced politician's voice was supposed to convey deep concern. An accomplished liar, he hit all the right notes to communicate sincerity and truth...

and self-control. Hugh Waltham wasn't the kind of guy who spilled the beans. He danced like a classical sword fighter, agile with a rapier, darting close for a touché and pulling back.

Not my style. Blake charged forward with a broadsword, hacking and thwacking. He wanted to demand information about Abigail's so-called accident and Jordan's incarceration at the Institute. This slick, cowardly political creep had watched while Jordan's wrists were slashed. Hugh Waltham deserved to be smeared with the cold, hard knowledge of his crimes, but Blake knew his satisfaction would be short-lived.

"I can't help you," he said. *Even if I could, I wouldn't.*

"Don't underestimate yourself," Hugh said. "Come over to the house. We'll talk."

"I've already left town. I'm on my way to visit a friend in Texas."

"I intend to stay in touch with you, Captain. What's your friend's name?"

"Telling you—or anybody else—wouldn't be right. This is a lady friend."

Hugh chuckled. "She's a married woman, isn't she? Well, well, Captain Delaney, you're not as innocent as you pretend to be. I'm not surprised. To paraphrase Eleanor Roosevelt: 'Marines have the cleanest bodies, the filthiest minds, the highest morale and the lowest morals of any group of animals I've ever seen.'"

"She finished that quote with one more sentence. 'Thank God for the US Marine Corps.'" *And don't you forget it.*

"We have more in common than both of us falling in love with Jordan. Trust me about this, Captain.

She'll hurt you just like she hurt me. You'd be wise to stay in touch."

He'd rather cuddle up with a nest of rattlesnakes. Blake straightened his shoulders and retraced his steps to the diner. "Don't count on it."

"Why not? Are you already committed to play for Team Jordan?"

"I'm on Team USA," Blake said, "dedicated to fighting for democracy, decency and human rights. Seems to me that you and I don't have one damn thing in common."

He ended the call with a sincere hope that he'd never hear Hugh Waltham's smooth, conniving voice again.

Chapter Nine

"Mom, wake up!"

"Come on, Mom, open your eyes!"

Jordan went from deep slumber to instant alert—a survival mechanism of all mothers who sensed their offspring needed them. From being curled up in the passenger seat with a parka tucked around her shoulders, she jolted awake. Her fingers drew into fists, ready for battle. Her posture straightened, and her feet planted on the floorboards. The car was parked at the side of a road with the headlights cutting through a thick wall of ponderosa pine and boulders.

She blinked. The skies above the horizon were streaked with magenta and coral. *Almost nightfall. When did that happen? I must have been asleep for hours.* The last thing she remembered was a lunch break at a taco shack in Fruita near Grand Junction.

The interior light in the Suburban went on. She saw Blake behind the steering wheel, then she peered into the back seat where her five-year-old twins were rolling their eyes like teenagers and giving her a hard time about being a lazybones. She cleared her throat. "Where are we?"

"Colorado," the boys shouted in unison. "In a forest. On a mountain."

"Ice Mountain," Cooper said, ever vigilant in reporting the details.

Squinting at Blake, she asked, "Why are we stopped?"

"We're less than a mile away from the cabin."

A chorus of cheers erupted from the back seat. Cooper said, "You've got to see this place. Blake's built it himself."

"Is that so?" She knew he hadn't.

"Yeah," Alex said. "A man's home is his castle."

"Did Blake teach you that?"

Before the boys could answer, he interrupted. "I called ahead to my buddy, Chester, who lives across the lake. Do you remember him?"

"Of course, I do." A friend of the family who'd known Blake since childhood, Chester had encouraged him to join the US Marine Corps and to purchase this cabin with another friend. She thought of Chester as a father figure for Blake, replacing his biological father who left before he was five.

Absent fathers seemed to be a recurring theme in her life, and she experienced a stab of guilt for causing her twins the same pain she'd felt. Her own dad had died when she was eleven. She shook her shoulders, not needing to think about death in the family…or among dear friends. "Why did you call Chester?"

"To get the cabin ready for us. I didn't want to walk into any surprises."

Her brain clicked into gear, and she realized that he was talking about a possible ambush. They'd already discussed his connection to this hideaway. Eleven years ago—just after his first deployment—Blake bought the cabin in partnership with a guy who put his name on the deed. His partner had been killed earlier this year. He left his share of the cabin to Blake who kept the taxes paid and managed the upkeep with help from his neighbor Chester but had never gotten around to legally changing the deed, which meant there was no official record of his ownership. No one, other than very close friends, knew about Blake's connection to this property on Ice Mountain. "And what did Chester tell you?"

"He opened up the cabin, and everything is A-OK. The toilet flushes. The heat is turned on. And he stocked the fridge with some basic groceries."

When she looked into the back seat, a genuine smile lifted the corners of her mouth. "What do you say, boys? Should we check out the cabin?"

While the kids shouted agreement, Blake eased the Suburban forward on the narrow, curving road through the forest. Excitement from the twins infected her as well. They were almost home safe. She'd pulled off the first part of her escape from Hugh and his minions, and that wasn't the only reason she was glad to be back to the cabin on Ice Mountain. It was here, seven years ago, that she'd spent an idyllic five days with Blake. They'd made love every night, talked about their dreams, laughed and hiked through the pine-scented forest until they were exhausted. She had seriously considered marrying him.

When the Suburban rounded a final curve, the shadows parted to reveal a two-story log cabin with a gently slanted, gabled roof of faded red shingles. The porch light cast a golden glow onto a covered porch that stretched across the first floor. Red hummingbird feeders dangled above the porch railings, and the tinkling sounds of wind chimes serenaded them.

He parked in the gravel drive to the right of the porch. The twins unfastened their seat belts but stayed in the boosters.

"Mom, Mom, Mom, can we get out?"

"Can we go, can we go?"

"Wait for us outside the front door," she said, "but yeah, you can go."

The back doors flung open, and they dashed through the trees.

"Why did you tell them to wait?" Blake asked.

"I seem to recall several security measures at this cabin, and I wanted to be sure the front door wouldn't explode when it was touched by unauthorized little fingers."

"Good point."

"There's a lot of other stuff I remember. Good stuff."

"Me, too." He gave her a grin. "During the five days and four nights we stayed here, I proposed marriage three times. Why did you turn me down, Jordan?"

"As you know, men and women are different."

"Agreed."

"When men fall in love, they're more romantic and less realistic than women. Most of the stories of unrequited love are about men who are pining away for the first woman they ever kissed or a great beauty seen from afar. On the other hand, women are down-to-earth and practical. They like to see bank statements and evidence of steady employment."

"You've given this a lot of thought," he said. "Did you write an article on the topic?"

She bobbed her head. "An interview with two sex therapists—a man and a woman. I agreed with the woman."

"Not surprised."

"Like her, I'm pragmatic. I looked at our relationship and evaluated. The sex was amazing. The same was true for the camaraderie. It was great to be with someone who could always make me laugh. However, we were both defined by our careers. I couldn't ask you to give up being a marine. And vice versa for me and journalism."

He pushed open his car door. "Things are different now."

What does that mean? Unfortunately, now wasn't the time for a deep discussion. On the porch, the boys were bouncing back and forth between the railing and the side of the log cabin. "We'd better let those two jumping beans go inside before they break the door down."

"FYI, there are no weird locking devices, but it'll take a minute for them to figure out the keypad system. If they get it wrong, we get blasted with an ear-splitting alarm."

She fell into step behind him. "Did the kids drive you up a wall while I was sleeping?"

"We were cool. I gave them a history lesson about Indigenous people and pioneers coming west. Cooper had a couple of stories I've never heard. Mostly from educational television."

He unlocked the front door and disabled the alarm using the keypad, which he promptly reactivated when they were inside. When she was here before, she had questioned him about the need for security, and he explained that since the cabin was vacant for long periods of time, he needed the alarm to scare off burglars. Any break-in also sent a phone notification to Chester, who could be at his front door in ten minutes. If she'd come here without him, the alarm would have been a problem, but now the precautions reassured her. Every extra ounce of protection was welcome.

Blake strode through the front room with the moss rock fireplace, a sofa, comfy chairs for reading and a long walnut dinner table with eight chairs. He directed the boys. "The kitchen is back there. My office is tucked away on the other side of the staircase, and the bathroom and washing machine are there, too. Upstairs, there are two bedrooms."

The floor plan took a moment to register in her mind. Two bedrooms meant one for the twins and a master for her and Blake. One bedroom, and she remembered one very comfortable king-size bed. When she'd first initiated this escape plan, he hadn't been part of the picture. Now, Blake stood front and center.

They hadn't talked about sleeping arrangements, and she didn't know what to say or how to react. Was it too soon for them to dive into the sack together? Was she expecting too much, pushing their relationship forward too fast? On the other hand, if they didn't sleep together very soon, she'd be overwhelmed by some very uncharacteristic leanings toward romantic love. *Hah! That's what I get for claiming I'm immune and don't get carried away.* She'd been so glib about her cool, pragmatic nature. In truth, the idea of lying beside him on the great, big bed sparked a fire in her belly. If she didn't get herself under control, she'd melt into a sloppy little puddle of unrequited lust.

BLAKE BELONGED HERE in his cabin on Ice Mountain. This was home.

He loved his mom and two half sisters, but their contact was minimal, and he hadn't lived with his family since he went to college on a football scholarship. With the twins walking on either side, he showed off the kitchen and returned to the staircase near the front door where their mother stood, frozen in thought. Her stillness worried him, and he was glad when she drifted toward the kitchen.

To the boys, he said, "Your bedroom is upstairs."

"Can we see it?"

"Sure, knock yourself out."

"I love this place," Alex announced as he clambered up the stairs.

"Me, too." Though he hadn't built the cabin, despite what Cooper thought, he'd added a two-car garage and done a ton of work on the septic system and the well. Running water and a flush toilet were two of the major reasons Chester had advised him to buy this three-acre property when it came on the market. Way back then, Blake hadn't understood the importance of water rights in Colorado and a well that could provide a steady flow. He'd grown up in Illinois, in cities where water was a given. Proudly, he continued the grand tour as the kids rejoined him and they went to the bathroom/laundry room.

"How come there's no bathtub?" Cooper asked.

"Real men like showers," Alex said.

From the front room, Jordan spoke up. "I like showers, too."

Instead of debating the question of which method got you cleaner, Blake launched into a lecture on water conservation that included not using too much water when you brushed your teeth, not washing clothes until you've got a full load and not taking a shower every day. "Not unless you're really dirty."

"Got it. Really dirty." Alex nodded. "I'm going to like living here."

Jordan appeared in the doorway. "It's a fantastic bathroom, but I like the kitchen better. Chester left us a selection of ham and cheese for sandwiches. And chips."

The boys ran toward the kitchen, and he joined Jordan in the narrow hallway. "Does the cabin live up to your memories?"

She gave him a quick hug and stepped back, putting distance between them. "I thought you were going to take down the wall between the kitchen and dining room to make a counter."

"A pending project." There was always something. "I'll unpack the car and put it away in the garage while you feed the kids."

"And then, we have something important to talk about."

He guessed she wanted to discuss plans for the investigation into her ex-husband's affairs. "You're going to start making lists, aren't you?"

"I always do. I need lists and schedules to stay on target."

"What's the number one item?"

"After dinner and getting settled, there's only one task for tonight." She turned her face away from him and studied a watercolor painting of a mountain lake that hung on the wall between the bathroom and the study. "We can talk about it later."

Obviously, she was hedging, and her unwillingness to bring up a troublesome issue bothered him. "Tell me now."

"Sleeping arrangements." She refused to look him in the eye. "There's only one king-size bed in the master bedroom, right?"

"Correct." He couldn't believe this was a big deal. Did she think he was going to jump her? Force her to have sex as payment for using his cabin? He shoved open the door to his study and pointed to the full-size, foldout sleeper sofa against the wall. "I'll bunk there."

Relief splashed across her face. Apparently, the idea of sleeping with him freaked her out. "That doesn't seem fair. I should take the sleeper. It's not long enough for your legs."

"I'll manage."

Her phone dinged, and she took it from her pocket. "A text from Spike."

The computer genius had taken his time getting back to her. For a moment, Blake dared to hope the message would be good news about Abigail's accident.

As Jordan stared at the screen on the cell phone, her face crumpled and a tear leaked from her eye. "She's dead."

Don't cry. Damn it, don't. Other tears spilled down her cheeks, breaking through barriers he wasn't aware he'd built and making him feel helpless. He hated to see her—or anybody else—weep. When he heard the twins yelling from the kitchen about sandwiches, he was grateful for the distraction. They'd found a bag of corn chips and bottles of a strawberry-flavored drink. He took a step in their direction. "Should I make sandwiches?"

"Stay with me." She passed him the phone. "My eyes won't focus. Read the rest of the text for me."

The tiny print covered most of the screen and dribbled onto another. Spike's precise details about contusions, concussions and internal brain bleed sounded like a medical examiner's report and made him wonder how an outside computer guy managed to access those records.

He skipped the painful details of her physical condition and summarized from the police report. "Her BMW broke through a guardrail and flew off the mountain road. Not wearing her seat belt, she was thrown from the car. Her injuries were fatal. She smelled like booze."

Jordan hiccupped a sob.

He continued, "The state highway patrol and the Flagstaff PD will investigate. As of now, they're calling her death an accident, possibly a DUI."

"What?" She swabbed at her eyes. "Abigail wasn't a heavy drinker. How could they make that kind of mistake?"

Blake suspected the police had been influenced by Waltham and his many contacts. In his mind, he could almost hear the smooth politico talking about the tragedy and bemoaning Abigail's heavy alcohol consumption. "Spike has two more bits of unrelated information.

I'm not sure how he taps into this stuff, but he's incredible."

"What does he say?"

"Number one: Hugh's security team, led by Gorilla Gruber, is working with Khaled. They're looking for the Prius in Las Vegas but haven't found the car."

"Nothing about Harvey? Or Emily and the chopper?"

"Not a peep."

"That's good. They haven't figured out how we left town." She dabbed at her eyes again. The tears were gone. "Do they mention San Francisco?"

"Spike says no."

"You said there were two bits."

"I don't know what this means." He held up the phone and read verbatim. "Retired squirrel makes nest in Aspen—a multi-million-dollar house is pricey for Rockwell from Flagstaff."

"I'll explain later," she said.

Before his eyes, her expression transformed. No more crying, her gaze hardened. She was a fierce huntress who had sighted prey. He almost felt sorry for Rockwell from Flagstaff...whoever that was.

Chapter Ten

After being separated from her kids for three months, Jordan enjoyed the relative normalcy of making a dinner of sandwiches and corn chips, unpacking the few items in their duffels and supervising while the boys took showers and brushed their teeth. She noticed tiny differences in their height and weight, scrutinized every new scrape or bruise and wondered if Alex had cut his own hair. Cooper showed signs of not sleeping well, with dark circles under his eyes, and he seemed to be squinting as if he needed glasses. Alex had perfected the embarrassed eye roll and developed a new habit of stubbornly sticking out his chin. Though she hadn't expected Hugh or Helena to directly abuse the kids, her ex-husband had never been a loving, nurturing father. The psychological injuries he inflicted would be more difficult to detect, but she knew the boys were hurt when their father dismissed them or ignored them or sternly demanded that they always, always, always be the best, the winner, first place.

In their second-floor bedroom of the cabin, Jordan tucked the twins under the heavy quilts, turned on night-lights and settled into a rocking chair under a

lamp to read a bedtime excerpt from *The Hobbit*, which
was the one item Cooper had chosen to bring with him.
The small, well-worn volume trembled in her hands as
she remembered. Before they fled from the mansion,
Abigail had been reading this book to the twins, using
different voices with dreadful British accents for each
of the characters. She'd been a good, loyal friend. If
only she'd listened to Jordan's warnings, things would
have turned out differently.

"Page sixty-three," Cooper said. "That's where Abigail stopped."

Of course, he kept track. Tolkien wasn't his favorite
but a close second to Harry Potter.

"Mom," Alex said, "is there really such a thing as
dwarves? Do they live in caves? Some of them might
be around here."

"We'll look."

When she started reading, Jordan didn't attempt to
mimic Abigail's high-spirited performance. Instead,
she dedicated every word to her friend's memory. *Oh,
Abigail, with your bright brown eyes and pixie haircut,
you'll be often mourned and deeply missed.*

In minutes, the twins succumbed to slumber. Jordan doused the lamp but kept the night-lights lit. If the
boys needed to go to the bathroom in the middle of the
night, they'd find the path leading down the staircase.

Mentally, she prepared herself for a confrontation
with Blake. He'd been insulted by her attitude about
sleeping together, and she was certain that he'd gal-
lantly insist on taking the sleeper bed in the study even
though his long legs would be cramped. She peeked into
the master bedroom, where he'd collapsed across the

king-size bed with his arms flung wide. *Out cold.* He'd already kicked off his boots and discarded his parka.

She crept onto the bed and gazed down at him. Stubble outlined his jaw. His short, golden-blond hair looked messier than she'd ever seen it. Breathing heavily, his lips parted, and she was tempted to lean down and kiss him until he was awake. *And then...what?* He'd kiss her back, and they'd be off to the races, even though the kids were sleeping right across the hall.

Instead, she scooted off the bed, pulled the denim-colored comforter over him and turned off the light. On her way out, she grabbed her duffel bag and carried it down the staircase into the study. After she showered, changed into flannel pajamas and converted the sofa into a sleeper, she stretched out on the bed—which left plenty of extra room for her tootsies—and told herself to relax. If she'd been a praying woman, she would have expressed a combination of gratitude and sorrow. Thanks for the successful escape from Flagstaff. And sadness about Abigail.

Her eyelids refused to close. She rolled onto her side and consciously tried to wish the tension away from her muscles, but she couldn't let go. Her fingertips danced on the pillowcase, writing an invisible list, and her toes twitched with a desire to run. *Settle down! You need your rest.* But her brain whirred and pinged in high gear. If she didn't get these details out of her head, she'd never fall asleep. *So much to do. So little time to do it.*

Bolting from the sleeper sofa, she slipped into cozy socks and her puffer jacket before she sat in the swivel chair behind Blake's desk. Still a bit chilly, she pulled up the hood on her deep purple coat and rubbed her cheek against the fake fur lining. Fingers spread on the desktop, she looked down at the flat, blank space before her. *Where to start?* Blake had a laptop she could use, and she had her flamingo flash drive, which she took from her duffel and centered on the desk. She flashed on a memory of handing over the penguin flash drive to Hornsby. She was lucky to have so many good friends.

Should she start by reviewing data? Not yet. Too complicated.

"Lists," she said aloud. "I need to set my agenda."

In the middle-right desk drawer, she found a yellow legal pad. In a clear mason jar that sat on the desk beside a stapler and a brass lamp, she saw an assortment of pens in different colors. *Perfect!* Color-coding her schedule made it easier to follow. For the easy tasks, she wrote with calming turquoise ink. First, she needed to go shopping to pick up winter clothes and other items for the kids. Then she'd take a trip to the grocery store for supplies and food. The page quickly filled. Even these everyday errands would be difficult since she didn't know the location of the nearest market and shops. Luckily, money was no object. When she first moved out of Hugh's mansion, she'd established a new identity complete with a driver's license, library card, bank account and credit cards to access her cash from savings.

She flipped to the next page in the legal pad and picked up the red pen, symbolizing urgency. Across the top, in capital letters, she wrote: "Accountant from Flagstaff."

Tim Rockwell, aka Rocky the Flying Squirrel, had been off the grid for the past several months. According to Spike, he was now in Aspen. She needed to meet with him, to convince him to testify against Hugh or, at least, to provide her with documentation to back up her accusations of fraud and money laundering.

She'd left the door to the study ajar in case the kids needed to find her, but Blake knocked anyway before opening it wider. "Jordan?"

"Come in," she said softly.

His gaze went from her hooded, purple jacket to her flannel jammies decorated with leaping reindeer to her fuzzy pink socks. "Are you trying to turn me on?"

She stuck a woolly foot into the air. "You like?"

"At least you're warm. Maybe even hot?"

"Want to find out?"

"I'll take a chance on getting burned." He licked his lips. "Where should I touch? What needs to be kissed?"

This was the closest they'd come to privacy since they'd met on the grounds behind the mansion. The twins were still nearby, tucked into their beds upstairs, but if Blake closed and locked the door to the study, they'd be mostly alone. She grinned. "Have you been stifling your lusty passion all this time?"

"Just trying to be appropriate." He took the legal pad from the desk and flipped to the first page. "How do you plan to do all this shopping?"

"Drive to a market?"

"I'm serious." He flopped onto the bed, which was— as she'd suspected—much too short for his six-foot-four-inch body. "We need to use precautions. The first rule should be to keep the twins secret. Anybody who sees those two little monkeys will remember them. Might as well send out an alert to Hugh and his minions: Pretty Mom and Twin Boys Shopping Near Aspen."

She knew he was right. Disguising herself wouldn't be all that hard. During the years she'd spent doing undercover research, she'd learned to alter her appearance with a change in hairstyle and makeup. She could easily pass for a mountain mama, but her adorable boys attracted too much attention. She suspected Blake, who was as muscular and handsome as a superhero, had a similar problem with being memorable, even though the ski bums and mountain men were a good-looking bunch. Blake had the additional problem of people in the area knowing him. If they went out together, he couldn't introduce her.

"I can manage a trip to the store on my own," she said.

"How about if we split the list? I'll do half in the morning. You finish in the afternoon."

"Fair enough." Several other projects fell under the category of urgent. Getting online and onto the dark web required expert instruction from Spike. Plus she needed to mine her old contacts and develop new ones. This investigation covered a lot more territory than her usual journalistic articles. She needed to provide the appropriate district attorney with enough evidence to convene a grand jury and charge Hugh.

"Rockwell from Aspen," Blake said, reading the second page of her list. "Is this the squirrel Spike was talking about?"

Immediately, she hushed him. "Keep your voice down. The less the twins know, the better."

"Agreed, but I'm not a kid, and I want a briefing on your current plan."

Not accustomed to working with a partner, she hated

to share her information. "Maybe tomorrow we'll find time to talk."

Lying on his side, he propped his head on his fist. His gaze narrowed as he studied her expression. "You don't trust me."

"Good guess."

"Not guessing," he said. "I know you better than you realize, Jordan. You can't hide your feelings from me."

"Is that so?" Nobody else could read her like Blake could. "What makes you think I'm holding back?"

"When you lie, the right corner of your mouth twitches. If you're hiding something, your eyelids lower a fraction of an inch."

"You sound like an interrogator. Or a profiler."

"I've learned some self-preservation techniques. I need guideposts to understand what's going on with you, and it's smart to analyze your microexpressions." His lips spread wide in a grin, and the dimples appeared to distract her. "Here's what happens after you change your mind about holding back: your eyes pop wide open in a flash. I like that look. It happens right before you unbutton your blouse and wriggle your jeans down your hips. Or your pajamas."

Not something she intended to do at the moment. "We should both go to sleep…in our separate bedrooms."

"Not until you tell me what's going on."

"I can't," she whispered. "It's too complicated. Hugh has committed scores of crimes ranging from larceny to money laundering to fraud, and maybe to murder. He has dozens of accomplices scattered across three or more western states. I don't even know where to start."

"At the beginning." Apparently, he had no intention of dropping this subject until he had answers.

"Let it go, Blake. It'll be easier for you to understand the big picture when I have the computer programs up and running."

He unfolded himself from the sleeper sofa, crossed the office and stood on the opposite side of the desk. "Here's the deal, Jordan—you're an amazing reporter. One of your best skills is breaking complex issues into logical bites. I want to know what we're up against. Talk to me."

"Not here." She clenched her jaw, determined to hold back. But resistance was futile. He was wearing her down. "I know the boys look like they're sound asleep, but they've got super-hearing, like bats. Even from upstairs, they can listen."

"And you don't want them to overhear and think you're bad-mouthing their pop."

"That's correct." If Hugh was guilty of half the crimes she suspected, that knowledge would be difficult for his sons to accept. She wanted to shield them from their father's evil.

Blake came around the desk and turned the swivel chair so she was facing him. He took her hand. "Come with me. We'll go outside to talk."

"And leave the kids here? Unguarded?"

"If anybody attempts to break in, an earsplitting alarm will sound."

"And if they open the door?"

"Same thing. Loud whooping alarm. I'm guessing your boys will love it." He tugged gently at her hand. "Come on, you're already wearing your parka."

She jammed her feet into sneakers, noticing that he'd already donned his boots. He grabbed his parka and slipped it on. "You're ready to go. Did you plan all along to take me outside?"

"The thought entered my mind."

At the front door, he disarmed the alarm system and set it to reengage in one minute, after they stepped onto the porch. In the stillness of the surrounding forest, the glow from the round, full hunter's moon lit the skies above the tall spires of trees and jagged granite rock formations. She saw no other lights. No neighbors in sight. No cars on the narrow dirt road at the base of the steep hill below the cabin.

She inhaled and exhaled with a sigh. The crisp breeze carried the scent of pine resin. A pleasant chill pushed inside her jacket, and she zipped up.

On the right side of the cabin, he found a winding path that led uphill to a clearing—a route she remembered fondly from their visit so many years ago. They'd made love in this small mountain glen, and life had seemed nearly perfect. At that time, she'd thought her experiences working for big-city newspapers and magazines combined with real-life moments in war zones had made her worldly, intelligent and capable of handling anything. *What a joke!* Though not helpless, she'd been naive.

Becoming the mother of twins had taught her more about life than any armed conflict or newsroom deadline barked by ferocious editors. Her deep, transformative love for the boys was unlike anything she'd felt before. She'd grown emotionally. The current threat from her ex-husband and the danger she now faced had forced her to mature in a different, more painful way.

She paced to the edge of the tree line where leaves on the low shrubs had turned yellow and crimson. Pivoting, she faced Blake—a muscular silhouette with moonlight tangled in his hair. "I'm a different woman now than I was seven years ago. It's not the same as when we were lovers."

"I know." When he walked slowly toward her, she noticed a hitch in his step. He continued, "I've spent a lot of my adult life in war zones, but I somehow believed that I was going to live forever. Confined in the hospital after we hit the IED, I shook hands with death. And it changed me."

She looked past him down the slope to the outline of the cabin where faint streaks of light glimmered through curtained windows. The idea of moving any farther away from the twins made her nervous. This was far enough. A circular firepit made of stones occupied the center of the clearing. A long wooden bench and a couple of tree stumps provided seating. Sitting, she faced the cabin. "It's peaceful here."

"We can't let ourselves get too comfortable." He prowled across a carpet of pine needles and twigs, pausing to peer into the darkness. "We may have eluded Hugh for the moment with the trip through Las Vegas and the unexpected drive to Colorado, but we can't underestimate him. He's dangerous."

"I know."

She didn't want to be reminded, but Blake was one hundred percent correct. Though momentarily comfy, she needed to plot her next escape route and to find somewhere safe for the twins. Though she hated to imagine a scenario where Hugh would hurt the children, she had to consider the possibility. If the choice came down to eliminating them or saving his own skin, she knew which option he'd pick.

A shiver trickled down her spine. Coming up with a future escape plan climbed to the very top of her list of priorities. She'd need a new color of ink for her legal pad. And she'd also need Blake's advice. He knew this land around his cabin intimately.

He sat on the bench beside her and lightly caressed her cheek. "I wish I could stay here with you all night, kissing those soft lips and getting to know the woman you've become. But I don't think we should be away from the boys."

"Thanks for understanding."

"Yeah, I'm a peach." He patted her cheek and pulled his hand away. "You've got fifteen minutes to tell me about your ex-husband's crimes and your investigation. I need to know, Jordan. We need to change this escape effort into a pursuit."

"Exactly." She liked the way that sounded.

"We'll put together enough evidence to make sure Hugh will never be able to come after you or the boys again."

"I'll be stalking him." The thought gave her a buzz of satisfaction.

"There's that look," Blake said. "You've made up your mind."

Not the first time she'd tracked down a story and stitched the pieces into a coherent whole. She knew the techniques of interview and research. She had the energy, drive and a whole lot of motivation.

Looking toward him, she opened her mind and started talking. "I'll start at the beginning. The first incident I uncovered was border fraud. Hugh used his political influence to open the border and allow weapons and contraband to flow across."

There it was: the tip of the iceberg. There was more, so much more, to come.

Chapter Eleven

Sitting on the wood bench at the edge of the forest, Blake tried not to be distracted by the glow of moonlight that played across Jordan's cheekbones and stubborn little jaw. It was hard for him to concentrate when she gazed at him with her enormous blue eyes, ringed by thick dark lashes. How could he think about anything other than how truly beautiful she was? *Get it together, dude. You're a marine, not a lovesick puppy dog.* He had to ignore his natural urges and pay attention.

"Are you listening?" she asked.

"Sure. Why wouldn't I be?"

"I want you to understand what we're up against, and I'm going to talk fast so we can go back inside and get some sleep. Agreed?"

"I'm ready for bed." *Not a lie.* In his opinion, going to bed was an excellent idea that didn't necessarily include sleep.

"Here goes."

She spewed a torrent of data—including names, dates and amounts of cash payments—showing how Waltham had arranged with state police and ICE officials to open a corridor for a Mexican cartel. Though

Blake didn't know much about how drugs were packaged and shipped, he had a high level of expertise when it came to weaponry. If Jordan's figures were correct, these semiautomatic guns, grenades and rocket launchers were enough to supply a small army.

"Wait." He held up his palm, halting this gush of information. "You've got plenty of evidence. Did you inform a prosecutor?"

"There are a couple of problems."

He assumed super-organized Jordan had efficiently labeled the obstacles. "Such as."

"I don't have clear chains of evidence to present in a court of law." She held up her index finger symbolizing number one. "That's because Hugh distances himself from the paperwork. Too much is hearsay. I've never actually seen the contraband weapons."

She popped up another finger. "Number two. My witnesses aren't about to come forward and talk to the feds."

He nodded. Betraying the cartel would be signing a death warrant. "What else?"

"Here's the biggie." She scowled. "I wanted to approach the attorney general's office in Arizona, but too many people on his staff were in Hugh's pocket. My ex knows everybody, and most of them owe him favors. The cops are no better. I can't very well hand him over to law enforcement when he's regularly making payoffs to many of them."

"Are you telling me that the entire legal system and all the police are corrupt?"

"Of course not. In spite of the rumors spread by Hugh and the guys in white coats at the Institute, I'm

YOU pick your books –
WE pay for everything.
You get up to FOUR New Books and TWO Mystery Gifts...absolutely FREE

Dear Reader,

I am writing to announce the launch of a huge **FREE BOOKS GIVEAWAY**... and to let you know that YOU are entitled to choose up to FOUR fantastic books that WE pay for.

Try **Harlequin® Romantic Suspense** books featuring heart-racing page-turners with unexpected plot twists and irresistible chemistry that will keep you guessing to the very end.

Try **Harlequin Intrigue® Larger-Print** books featuring action-packed stories that will keep you on the edge of your seat. Solve the crime and deliver justice at all costs.

Or TRY BOTH!

In return, we ask just one favor: Would you please participate in our brief Reader Survey? We'd love to hear from you.

This FREE BOOKS GIVEAWAY means that your introductory shipment is completely free, even the shipping! If you decide to continue, you can look forward to curated monthly shipments of brand-new books from your selected series, always at a discount off the cover price! Plus you can cancel any time. Who could pass up a deal like that?

Sincerely

Pam Powers

Pam Powers
For Harlequin Reader Service

not completely paranoid. However…" She paused. "It's really hard to tell the good guys from the baddies. I didn't want to provoke all-out warfare between them."

As the pieces to this puzzle snapped into place, his brain finally got into gear. Blake understood betrayal and had encountered many such obstacles in combat zones. In addition to traitors in the military and among outside contractors, he faced tribal warlords who could be unpredictable and disloyal. "It's the same everywhere."

"They're all out for themselves."

"And whoever has the biggest war chest gets to call the shots. What about contacting the FBI or DEA?"

"Too much of a risk. If I got unlucky and reported Hugh to one of his sleazebag cronies, I'd be in deep trouble."

"When did you first become aware of the border fraud?"

"About a year and a half ago." She rose from the bench and took a step away from him. "Earlier than that, I had suspicions but not solid evidence. Turning in my husband was an extreme measure. I hesitated. I didn't want to destroy my family."

"What changed your mind?"

"Hugh beefed up his security force." She paced across the front of the clearing and looked down at the cabin. "Having so many armed guards around the house scared me."

"Hugh must have thought somebody else was after him."

"For a while I thought Abigail's husband, Stanley Preston, was on Hugh's enemy list because he was involved in border issues and protested the unfair treatment of immigrants. He and Hugh are both dynamic men. I could see them facing off with each other. But I read the situation wrong. Stanley, a defense attorney, was part of a team that represented a high-ranking member of the cartel."

"He and Hugh were working together."

"I think so." She took a step toward him, then pivoted in a graceful pirouette and stepped back toward the cabin. Her movements were part of a complicated dance, balancing her desire to find the truth with her love for her children.

He asked, "When you started digging, what did you find out?"

"After wasting a lot of time reading Hugh's bank statements and monitoring his computer records, I was on the verge of giving up. Don't get me wrong. I found a ton of wrongdoing, including the Las Vegas connection where Hugh was laundering cash payoffs through the casinos, but all my investigating seemed futile. Even if I produced enough evidence to have Hugh convicted of fraud, extortion and embezzlement, his sentence wouldn't amount to much more than a fine and less than five years in a white-collar prison."

"He'd lose his influence as a political consultant."

"And he couldn't run for the US Senate." She threw up her hands. "Not a big deal for him, especially if he'd stashed away a small fortune in offshore accounts. Anyway, I almost dropped the whole thing."

"What stopped you?"

"His crimes went from bad to worse. He transformed from being a greedy, money-grubbing sleaze to becoming nearly demonic. I swear there were times when I could almost see his horns and tail. I had to find a way to stop him. For myself…my kids…and others."

Her gestures became more vigorous as she built to a climax. Gently, he asked, "Are you all right?"

"If I'd acted more quickly… If I'd been braver…" She stopped moving and stood completely still. "I'll never know if he actually wielded the knife, but Hugh was responsible for the bloody murder of a young woman. Her name was Bianca Hernandez. She was sixteen and pregnant with twins."

Jordan's legs collapsed. Shuddering, she sank onto the bench beside him. Her head drooped forward on her chest. Her arms wrapped around her middle. When she'd been outlining Hugh's participation in fraud, embezzlement and money laundering, she'd been disgusted and outraged. The murder of a young woman was a heavier emotional burden. Blake wanted to comfort her, to touch her and tell her that everything was okay. But when he reached toward her, she flinched.

She spoke so quietly that the rustling of wind through the pines nearly swallowed her words. "I have to stop him before he kills again."

"How did you learn about what happened to Bianca?"

"Investigating the border fraud. I started hearing rumors about women being funneled into a service that provides cheap labor, maids and nannies. These women, mostly undocumented, are promised employment when they cross the border. They aren't told that the wages are substandard or, in some cases, nonexistent. Basically, they're recruited to become domestic slaves."

"That sounds like the type of article you used to really get into." He recalled her zeal and youthful enthusiasm. "You used to love tracking down sources, interviewing victims and making a difference for people who have no one else to speak for them."

He'd been proud of her investigative journalism. Sure, Jordan did fluff pieces on purebred dog shows and celebrity spats. But she had a conscience and a solid focus on right and wrong. When she sank her teeth into a story, she held on like a pit bull.

"Needless to say, Hugh wasn't thrilled when I told him that I intended to write about Bianca's death. He knew me well enough to avoid making an outright demand for me to drop my investigation. Instead, he manipulated me by putting me in touch with the medical examiner and his handpicked sheriff, who headed up the team of detectives." Ruefully, she shook her head. "I had to beg the ME for the autopsy photos. And he still managed to leave things out. He and the sheriff were hiding evidence and leading me down the wrong path. Also, they made it clear to everyone involved that I was a bored politician's wife looking for a cheap thrill as a journalist."

"A cupcake," he said.

She grinned. "That's what the guys in your platoon used to call me—cupcake, sweetie pie, Jordy the jelly bean."

"Until you confronted and disarmed a teenage punk armed with a Kalashnikov."

"Good times," she said sweetly. "And I understand why I'm not taken seriously. I show up with a recorder, a smile and a pocketful of questions. Then I go home to my safe, warm life. It doesn't look like I've got skin in the game. Reporting on a crime isn't the same as being victimized."

Her recent experiences—the life-threatening attack by Gruber and incarceration at the Institute—must have given her a different perspective. Now, she was the victim. Desperate enough to dodge outside the boundaries of the law.

"Was anyone arrested for Bianca's murder?"

"Unsolved." She shivered as though the cool, crisp night had turned ice-cold. "I met her sister, who had also been trafficked, and told her that I'd get justice for Bianca and her unborn twins. I never make promises like that, but I couldn't let go. I identified with this young woman who was five months into her pregnancy. I remembered the miraculous joy I'd felt. To have that power snuffed out is just so damn wrong."

When he met her gaze, he saw strength and determination. At the same time, she'd begun to fidget as she stared at the cabin. "You want to get back to the boys, don't you?"

"I do, but there's more to tell."

"It'll wait," he said. "Our basic plan for tomorrow includes gathering supplies and establishing our emergency escape routes through the forest."

"Yes."

Without further comment, she approached him, grabbed the front of his parka and went up on tiptoe to kiss him full on the mouth. The pressure of her lips against his was demanding. She wanted more. And yet, she shoved him away. Blake was a little bit stunned and a whole lot confused…in a good way.

AFTER BLAKE FED the twins breakfast and listened to the many reasons why—including a magic recipe—their mom's pancakes were better than his, he decided it was time to establish their emergency escape routes in case they were tracked down and surprised by Gruber. The boys needed to be educated about security. In the front room, he went to a window and placed the flat of his hand against the pane.

"Do you see how gentle I'm being?"

"So what?" Alex demanded.

"If I press harder, I set off the alarm."

Cooper frowned. "Is there some kind of force field or something?"

"Cool," Alex said. "Can you make the window explode?"

"I'm trying to show you something about the alarm system," he said, stating the obvious. "If somebody or something breaks the glass or pushes too hard against the interior or exterior, it sets off a loud alarm."

"Can I do it?" Alex marched toward the window with both hands sticking straight out. "How hard do I hit the window?"

"Stop right there," Blake said. "Your mom is still sleeping. Do you really want to wake her with a screeching blast from a security alarm?"

The boys gave identical nods and grins. "Yeah, let's do it."

"Bad idea." They weren't listening to him. He was losing control. "Get over here by the door. I'll show you how to lock and unlock without engaging the alarm."

"Then can we set it off?"

"Why would you want to do that?"

"A joke on mom," Cooper said. "She's really goofy before she has coffee."

"Have you got coffee in the kitchen?" Alex asked.

Blake recalled the conversation from yesterday. "No caffeine for you guys. But yes, there's a fresh pot made."

They exchanged a sneaky glance that turned all wide-eyed and innocent when they looked up at him and asked him to please explain the alarms. The five-year-old boy who lived in Blake's memory warned him not to trust these two. He really wanted to believe that his adult self was in charge.

He illustrated the use of the keypad that was just reachable for their three-foot-ten-inch height, which Jordan said was tall for their age. "Within sixty seconds of opening or closing the door, you tap these numbers into the pad. If you fail to do so, an alarm sounds from here, and an emergency call is placed to my buddy, Chester, who can be here in ten minutes."

"How come?" Alex asked. "Why would your buddy rush over here?"

"To protect the house or to help me deal with intruders."

"Do you get many burglars?" Cooper asked.

"Few. This cabin is remote." He grabbed the opportunity for a teachable moment. "It's better to be overprepared instead of not being ready for a break-in or an attack."

"Why would you get attacked?" Alex demanded.

"You know," Cooper said. "That's why Dad has all those dumb security guards. He's got enemies. Do you, Blake? Are there bad guys after you?"

Rather than attempting to explain that the bad guys worked for their father, he sidestepped the question. "Let's go over the procedure for the alarm again."

They tried it once and then again. He sent the boys out to the porch to open the door and disarm the alarm. The twins caught on to the procedure more quickly than some of the newbie recruits he'd worked with. "I think you've got it."

"One more time," Alex said. "I want to be sure."

"I'm okay," Cooper said as he went toward the kitchen.

In spite of a nagging sense that he was being played, Blake took a step back from the front door. "Go for it."

Alex opened the door and took his position in front of the keypad. He shifted his weight from one foot to the other. "Um, how long before the alarm goes off?"

"Sixty seconds," Cooper yelled from the kitchen.

Alex bobbed his head up and down, then gave an elaborate shrug. "Uh-oh, I think I forgot the code."

"Ten seconds to go," Cooper said as he returned to the front room. "That's eight…seven…six…"

Alex spread his arms like a soccer goalie, keeping Blake away from the keypad. Their plan to "accidentally" activate the alarm siren became apparent. *Fine, let the little monsters have their fun.*

The alarm screamed with shrill, piercing notes that reminded him of a barn owl and a howler monkey in a blender. Alex covered his ears and chortled. After a moment, Cooper joined in. Blake turned off the alarm and braced himself. Disaster struck.

The beast had been awakened. Wearing her colorful reindeer jammies, Jordan leaped into the front room and landed in a karate pose that resembled the cat leg stance. Her curly hair stood up in tangles on her head. She kicked in all four directions, shouting a fierce accompaniment to each movement. "Hai. Hai-hai-hai."

Blinking repeatedly, she glowered from Blake to the boys and back again. The twins reacted. Alex and Cooper stood on either side of her and pointed her toward a padded walnut chair that matched the long table. As soon as she was seated, Cooper placed a ceramic coffee mug on the table in front of her.

"Sorry, Mom." Alex patted her shoulder. "Blake made us do it. He thought it'd be funny to wake you up."

Just like that, the kid threw him under the bus. Not a smart move. Blake knew his way around Ice Mountain and had a few tricks of his own.

This incident represented a lesson learned. Never get into a squabble with twins. They were twice as hard to defeat. When they were five years old, they were twice as cute.

Chapter Twelve

Jordan hated pranks. She didn't know whether to applaud Blake's ability to bond with her children or to treat him like another kid. Before she could sort out her reaction, he stepped forward.

"Earlier, the boys learned about the keypad alarm system," he said in the mature voice that befitted a big, handsome marine. "I have more plans for this morning."

"Tell me."

"We'll explore the terrain surrounding the cabin before we check out nearby caves and hideouts."

"Looking for dwarves," Alex explained.

"I'm in," she said. Her head was still fuzzy from the rude awakening, but she needed to be a part of this effort. She took a gulp from her mug. The strong, fragrant coffee warmed her throat. "Give me a minute." She sipped again. *Come on, caffeine, do your stuff.* "If you boys pay attention and do as you're told, I might be inclined to believe that the wailing banshee alarm was an accident. I just might forgive you."

"Okay," Cooper said, "we're ready to go."

"Don't push me." The three of them took a backward

step, giving her space and enough time to guzzle her coffee and get ready. Still not caught up on sleep, she'd come back to the cabin last night and set up Blake's computer. Without using internet or Wi-Fi, she plugged in her fat flamingo flash drive and read over the notes, witness statements and documents she'd already compiled. Her review had been worth the exhaustion. She was on the trail to solving Bianca's murder.

She took another slug of coffee, keeping Bianca at the forefront of her thoughts. Jordan didn't dare call or text the murdered woman's sister for follow-up. Not after what had happened to Abigail. She didn't want to cause another murder.

It occurred to her to approach the Flagstaff PD, but they hadn't helped when Hugh had her locked up at the Institute. Not one single officer would listen to her.

She needed Blake's clear thinking on this problem. With a clumsy gesture, she waved him toward her. "Please come with me."

The twins chuckled and hooted about how he was in big trouble. Their giggles ceased when she shot them a glare. "Don't go outside. Don't get in trouble."

"Okay, Mom."

"I mean it. Don't go outside." She glanced toward the kitchen. "I see a mess on the counter. Clean up the dishes. Now."

While they rushed to obey her order, she pulled Blake into the study. She pointed to the chair behind the desk, indicating he should sit, and she closed the door. "I don't want to leave the kids unsupervised for long, so listen up."

"Yes, ma'am."

BLAKE COVERED HIS mouth with his hand, hiding a grin. Clearly, Jordan wasn't in the mood for more goofing around. He considered himself lucky that she hadn't whipped out her titanium baton and pummeled him from top to toe for the stunt he'd allowed the twins to pull.

"I need to show you something." She took another swig of her coffee. "It's a vital piece of evidence about Bianca's murder, but I don't know how to use it to best effect."

"Are you sure you can't go to the police?"

"Positive."

She turned on the laptop. Without a connection to the internet, the small device was basically a word processor and storage space for the information she'd gathered and stored on her fat flamingo flash drive. Blake was glad she'd saved this data. Maybe her story would have a happy ending after all.

She clicked on an icon labeled ME. "This is information from the Flagstaff medical examiner's office about Bianca's autopsy."

"Can you trust the ME?"

"You'd think so." But she scoffed. "Hugh instructed him to work with me on my so-called story assignment, and he complied…to an extent. Here's an example of his cooperation: he did DNA testing on the unborn twins and told me that there were no matches."

"Which you don't believe."

"No way. The paternity issue could be a motivation for Bianca's killing. I'm not sure Hugh's DNA is on file, but I could certainly provide a toothbrush or hair samples."

He nodded. "If Hugh was the father, he'd want Bianca out of the way."

"Or it could have been any of his cohorts. Hugh would have been doing them a favor by eliminating this inconvenient young woman." She sipped more coffee and shrugged. "I've found my best contacts in law enforcement are the tribal police at the Navajo reservation. Unfortunately, they didn't have tribal jurisdiction for Bianca's murder, not to mention that those officers are massively overworked. They don't have the time or resources to mess around with a cold case that's over two years old."

From outside the study, he heard the twins dashing across the hardwood floors and arguing loudly while telling each other to keep quiet. "Should I go check on them?"

"Yes." She took a final sip and held out her mug. "And bring me more caffeine."

When he stepped into the front room, he saw the two curly-haired kids studying the keypad alarm. The last thing their mom had told them was not to go outside. In a gravelly voice, he reinforced that order. "Don't even think about it. Don't go outdoors. Got it?"

Unimpressed with his growl, they bounced up to him. "Is Mom done yet?"

For a moment, he was tempted to use the roar he'd perfected after years of giving orders to newbie recruits. Then he remembered that these were five-year-old puppies, not devil dog marines. "As soon as she's done, I'll tell you."

He took her mug into the kitchen and filled it. When he returned to the combination living room/dining area, he pulled open a drawer in the lower section of a breakfront and took out several rolled and folded papers. "These are maps," he said as he placed them on the long, walnut table. "Be careful with them. Don't tear them up or write on them. I want you to study them and figure out which ones apply to our current location."

With the kids momentarily occupied, he returned to the study where Jordan had seated herself in his swivel chair. She stared intently at the computer screen. Without turning her head, she said, "It took me a long time and a lot of luck to put this evidence together. I hope it makes a difference."

"How about the FBI? We could contact them." He placed the fresh mug of coffee on the desktop beside the mouse. "Didn't you tell me that Bianca was victimized by traffickers? That's the feds' jurisdiction. Maybe her murder can be used to dismantle the forced labor enterprise."

"It's a possibility, but we've got to be careful about who we tell. According to my research, this isn't a sloppy operation. The name used by the traffickers has changed a couple of times, and the paperwork is almost nonexistent, making it nearly impossible to uncover the identities of men like Hugh who skim a percentage off the top."

"How does their operation work?"

"Back in Flagstaff, while I pretended to be a good little politician's wife, I heard about this 'employment service' from another of the wives, the ex-model Sierra, who has a full staff of household help and two nannies for her three kids. She described an extortionist's dream where you first pay a lump sum, a portion of which is supposedly passed on to your newly hired employee. If you're still happy after six months, you pay again. All cash, no questions."

"What's the name they're currently using?"

She looked up and gave him a sad smile. "I can't remember. Let me think. It'll come to me."

"Chester has a couple of contacts in the FBI, former marines. Men we can trust." He hoped she would agree to calling in outside investigators and stepping out of the direct line of fire. If not for her own safety, she needed to think of the kids. "Show me your new evidence."

She turned the computer screen so he could see. "These are autopsy photos of Bianca from the ME's office. I asked if I could take photos of my own, but he refused. To get these copies, I had to beg and plead."

Though battle-hardened, Blake felt a queasy tremor in the pit of his gut. Bianca was so young, only sixteen, and so vulnerable. Before the autopsy surgeon made the V-incision on her chest, he photographed the lacerations on her body. A slash across her breasts. Another on her abdomen. There was an X at the base of her throat, like a signature. "You said he used a machete. Is that right?"

"A weird choice for somebody living in Flagstaff."

"Not if he came from a cartel in a jungle area."

"The marking at her throat looks too delicate to be a machete," she said. "And take a look at this."

She zoomed in on the photographs taken of wounds inflicted at the victim's wrists. Horizontal slicing crisscrossed the veins and arteries. Blake squinted at the photo. "Not an efficient murder method. The carotid or femoral would bleed out more quickly. These wrist lacerations could take up to fifteen minutes before death was assured."

"Does it look like a machete wound?" she asked.

"I'm not an expert, but the width of the blade appears to be finer than a heavy-duty hacking tool. And then, there's this." He pointed to the screen. "At the end of the smooth slice, there appears to be a jagged nick. You might get that pattern using a hunting knife with a serrated edge below the tip."

He watched as she braced her elbow on the desktop and carefully removed the colorful, braided bracelet that circled a wide portion of her wrist. Her bared skin revealed a scar that was identical to the one on Bianca's arm. The scar beneath the second bracelet on the other arm matched the first. Those lacerations were given to her by Ray Gruber after he knocked her out with the stun gun.

Blake wanted to believe the scars indicated proof positive, but he said, "It's not an unusual style of blade—could belong to someone else."

Her gaze locked with his. She unfastened the top buttons on her jammies to reveal Gruber's signature X below her clavicle. "What are the odds?"

"This looks like solid evidence," he said. "And it's another reason for Hugh and Gruber to come after you."

The more evidence they uncovered, the more motivation the bad guys had for eliminating Jordan. They needed to think seriously about finding a safer place for the kids to hide out. He wanted to believe he and Jordan could protect them, but the odds weren't in their favor.

IN THE BATHROOM, Jordan washed her face, dragged a brush through her hair and checked her reflection in the mirror above the sink. In spite of the ever-present danger, she didn't look too bad. Her eyes weren't bloodshot, and she had a bit of color in her cheeks. She scowled at herself, trying to remember. *What was the phony employment service called?* She remembered Bianca's sister telling her, but the name wouldn't come clear.

She retreated to the study to get dressed. Today, she'd text information about the trafficking operation to Spike. Maybe he could figure it out. He was supposed to be in touch with an update on Rockwell in Aspen. Finding that evil squirrel and his stash of nuts was top priority. The name came to her in a flash: B and W Employ. She'd thought of the initials standing for "Bad" and "Worse," and she needed to track down connections to that supposed business.

When she emerged, she wore sneakers, jeans and a coral turtleneck under a lightweight khaki jacket—totally appropriate for hiking this morning and shopping this afternoon. She found the three guys sitting at the dining room table. Blake had spread a topographical map of the area that showed towns, landmarks and highways.

Alex motioned for her to join them. "Mom, take a look. It's old-fashioned."

For once, Cooper agreed with him. "Why would anybody use this instead of GPS?"

"Harry Potter has maps," she said defensively. "And the hobbits."

"But that's not real life," Alex said as if he knew.

"Maps are a good way to get an overview," Blake said. "Remember when I told you about the Tiger Squad? One time they parachuted out of a Cessna 208 Caravan into enemy territory and had to find their way to safety.

Suppose you boys went skydiving into the forest at the edge of this mountain." He pointed to the map. "How would you find your way to this cabin?"

"I'd use my cell phone," Alex said. "If Mom would get one for me."

"The cabin isn't listed under regular addresses in your GPS. All you've got is this map." Blake leaned back in his chair. "See if you can figure out where this cabin is located, based on the highways, towns and geographical features."

"That's a great exercise." Jordan leaned over the table and quickly realized that she was as lost as the twins. "You're going to have to give us more clues."

"When we drove here, we turned south off the interstate at Glenwood, then west, then south again."

She rotated the map until she had the directional marker pointing toward north at the top of the paper.

"This way," Alex said. With his finger, he traced the thick line for I-70.

"You got it," she said. "After going south on route 82, we turned west."

"Just before this town that starts with a *C*," Alex said. "Here's a curvy road. If this was on a computer, we could zoom in and get details."

"You catch on quick." Though Alex had always been good with spatial relationships, she was wowed by his swift, easy comprehension of mapping. "Have you done anything like this before? Maybe on the internet?"

He shrugged his skinny shoulders, but Cooper stepped up to fill in the blanks. "Alex plays that dumb computer game all the time. It's about carts and graphs."

"Cartography," Alex corrected.

"Impressed," Jordan said. "This is useful knowledge."

Cooper nudged against her and pointed to the elaborate directional marker above the legend of the map. "What's this?"

She explained how the marker, called a compass rose, showed the four directions and gradations in between. "You can design one for yourself."

Now Cooper was enthralled. "How do I know which way is north?"

"I thought you might ask," Blake said as he dug into his jeans pocket and pulled out two circular metal cases in army green. "These are military lensatic compasses. Flip open the lid. The needle always points north."

Jordan was glad he'd found two compasses and pleased to see the boys asking so many questions. Learning about these "old-fashioned" navigational instruments felt more real and solid than accessing directions on the computer. When she needed the internet, she loved it. Other times—like now—she enjoyed being off the grid.

Eventually, they solved the puzzle of finding the cabin by triangulating the turnoff from the highway and following a squiggly line that was Chipmunk Creek. She checked her watch. It was 8:45 a.m. Blake had planned to leave at 10:30 to do shopping for a couple of hours. Her turn to shop was from 2:00 until 4:00 p.m. The schedule made her feel grounded, and she'd learned something valuable while studying the map.

The location of the cabin was closer to Aspen than she'd thought. Though shopping at the acclaimed ski resort would undoubtedly be more costly, the proximity to Rockwell enticed her. Maybe she'd go there first, to get an idea of where he lived and what kind of security he used. Discovering the connection with the scars encouraged her to move forward with her investigation. The solution felt closer than ever before.

Chapter Thirteen

When they left the cabin, the boys showed Jordan how to use the keypad, proving to her that the earlier "accidental" alarm had been very much on purpose. Though she could have scolded, she didn't want to ruin the happy mood of hiking together and being outdoors. Blake led the way up the slope to the clearing where they'd gone last night. The twins dashed around the edges of the clearing and circled the firepit.

"Can we build a fire?"

"And cook weenies?"

Ignoring a plethora of demands and questions, Blake said, "Okay, I want you to use your compasses to find a path that goes northeast."

After a couple of false starts, they scampered down a trail, passed a grove of gold-leafed aspen and went deeper into the woods. She strolled beside Blake. The earthy scents of the forest comforted her. After being sequestered in the Institute, she felt lighthearted and free. Sunlight warmed her cheeks. The beautiful, blue-sky autumn day almost made her forget the peril hanging over them.

"I like the way you're handling this," she said, looking up at Blake. "You're teaching them an escape route without being scary."

"We'll follow these paths every morning until the directions are stuck in their memories. They're good kids. Smart."

"In terms of more aggressive protection," she said, "are you prepared?"

"If that's a roundabout way to ask if I have weapons, the answer is… Oh. Hell. Yes."

"Not surprised."

"Four hunting rifles and two handguns, all of which are locked in my gun safe except for my Glock, which I slept with under my pillow last night."

Her feelings about guns seesawed back and forth. As a young woman growing up with a single mother in Boston, she wasn't much interested in weapons. When she started in journalism, guns equated in her mind with street violence, and she favored gun control. That attitude changed. While embedded with the military in combat zones, she understood the vital function of weaponry in self-preservation. She learned to shoot with handguns and rifles but frankly preferred her titanium baton and karate moves. Her latest stance was the result of being the mother of energetic twins. Her brain fixated on the statistics for accidental shootings and gun deaths for kids under eighteen in 2021. It was over 5,200 in the United States. In many situations, guns were necessary, but she didn't like them.

"I'd prefer to keep the guns away from the boys," she said.

He nodded. "I hadn't planned on target practice."

"They get into everything." Ahead of them on the

path, the twins had come to a fork. They checked their compasses before deciding to go right and head uphill. "I can't turn my back on them for a second."

"I know what you mean."

She also knew that he had an awareness of safety and how guns should be used. Still, she couldn't stop herself from asking, "What if the boys stumbled across your Glock when you weren't looking?"

"I'm always looking."

"Really? I mean, do you know where your gun is right now?"

"In a concealed holster fastened to my belt at the small of my back." He brushed back his untucked flannel shirt to show her. "If Gruber attacks on this trail, my fire power isn't much good if it's locked in a safe. FYI, I'm also carrying a hunting knife and a switchblade."

She sighed. "I keep forgetting that you're no stranger to violence."

"I am now and always will be a battle-ready marine."

"Exactly what I need." She dropped her voice to a soft, intimate level. "More than that, you're exactly what I want."

Up ahead on the path, the boys were waving and shouting. "We'd better catch up to them," Blake said, "before they tear the mountain apart."

On a ridge above the trail, they'd located the entrance to a mine that was closed off by rough, weathered boards. Though not readily visible from the path, Jordan had the feeling that this was the destination Blake had intended for them to find. Her impression deepened when he unzipped the pack slung across his shoulders and took out four LED headlamps with elastic straps.

He passed a headlamp to her. "You're going to need this."

Not thrilled, she dangled the headgear between her thumb and forefinger. "Do you remember how I feel about dark, enclosed spaces?"

"Claustrophobia," he said. "Sorry, Jordan, but you've only got two choices. Either you get over it or you explain to the kids."

He joined the twins outside the mine, handed them the headlamps and showed them how to put them on and adjust the straps.

"Where did you get this stuff?" Alex asked.

"Some are gifts from Chester who likes to go caving, which is also called spelunking."

Cooper laughed. "Spelunking? That's a funny word."

"The headlamps are handy to see where you're going at night when you want to keep your hands free, like when you're hunting or fishing after dark."

Very little about caving or nighttime hunting appealed to her, but her sons were observing Blake with something akin to hero worship. He had headlamps and compasses, not to mention the holstered Glock and switchblade, which he hadn't shown them. She didn't want to be the sissy who was scared to go into the mine, but she couldn't ignore the involuntary flush of apprehension that raised her core temperature. Under her light jacket, she'd begun to sweat.

Blake pointed to the thick boards blocking the gaping entrance. "If you ever see another boarded-up mine, do not enter. You got that? It's not safe. This place is special. Chester and I checked it out, reinforced the supports and made it secure. It's a tricky route, meant to slip into and come out of."

"What about dwarves?" Cooper asked. "They work in mines. Is this a gold mine?"

"I'm not sure. All the ore that was there has been removed."

"So…no dwarves?"

"Not that I know of."

He went to the side of the entrance and pushed aside a clump of sage and juniper to reveal the edge of a long board. He pulled and twisted until there was a space just large enough for a regular-sized person to slip through. Jordan guessed it would be a tight squeeze for extra-large Blake.

Cooper echoed her thought. "Blake's too big. He's not going to fit."

She gave a nervous laugh. "You might be right about that."

"No problem. I'll go first and check it out." Blake turned on his headlamp, dropped into a squat, ducked under the boards and disappeared into the darkness. From inside, he called out, "Who's next?"

Jordan dragged her feet. She was content to wait outside and cheer for them when they emerged. For her, the spelunking wasn't going to happen. She hugged both of her brave boys. Her job was to protect them, not the other way around. "You go ahead. I'll see you on the other side."

After the kids darted inside, she adjusted the shrubs so the opening into the mine shaft wouldn't be obvious. From inside the cave, she heard the echo of Blake's deep voice. "This way. Keep to the right."

Stepping away from the mine entrance, she found a comfortable seat on a granite rock and tilted her head back. Sunshine poured over her like a soothing balm, and all her senses came alive. The breeze tickled. She heard the sounds of the forest. The temperature had begun to cool. She tasted the approach of winter and snow.

This time, claustrophobia won. What was that quote? "Discretion is the better part of valor." She didn't need to take unnecessary risks.

JUST BEFORE LUNCHTIME, Blake returned from the market with groceries, miscellaneous supplies and a rotisserie fried chicken. After they ate, Jordan left the twins with him and took the car for her turn at a general merchandise store to purchase clothes and office supplies. With the skies clouded over and the cool weather sliding toward cold, she needed to make sure the twins were prepared—with boots, mittens, hats and jackets—for the impending snowfall. During the brief time she'd spent in Colorado, she'd experienced sudden weather changes, and Blake assured her that October wasn't too early for a blizzard. While he'd been shopping, she and the twins took advantage of the still-temperate day to hike along Chipmunk Creek, a twisty little stream, too shallow for fishing, that led through the forest to Paddington Lake, named for one of the first settlers in the area.

The twins had spotted the short dock at the water's edge where a couple of rowboats were moored. If they'd had more time and less urgency, she would have immediately agreed to take them out on the lake. But the threat of danger crept closer with every passing minute. She couldn't let her guard down.

Earlier, she'd received a text message from Spike indicating activity from Khaled. The casino owner blamed Hugh for her investigation and decided to pursue his own search for her. Dissent among the bad guys seemed like good news for her. If they bickered with each other, they'd be less likely to worry about evidence she might be gathering. One of them might even decide to turn on the other, giving evidence of wrongdoing in exchange for a lighter sentence. As she drove toward the turnoff near Carbondale, she worried that Khaled might stumble across information about Emily. Would it be smart to toss a bit of misdirection into his path?

She pulled the Suburban over onto the shoulder and texted that question to Spike. The response from him was lightning quick. He had two more tidbits of information. First of all, Khaled and some of his men had flown on a private jet out of Harry Reid International Airport at dawn. Their destination was unknown. Jordan breathed a sigh of relief. If the gang from the Magic Lamp wasn't searching in Vegas, Emily the chopper pilot wasn't on their radar. Secondly, Spike texted the address for Tim Rockwell in Aspen.

When she hadn't known the precise location, the idea of tracking down Rocky had been too vague. Now, she knew where the squirrel was holed up. If she finished her shopping fast, she might have time to check out his house before she rushed back to the cabin.

Merging into the minimal traffic, she remembered the topographical map on Blake's dining room table. Up ahead was a fork in the road. A left turn, heading north, took her toward Glenwood Springs. To the right was Aspen, only about thirty miles away. *Tempting.*

She did the math in her head. A detour into Rocky's neighborhood would add about an hour and a half to the time she'd allotted for shopping. Too long to be away from the boys. And she wanted Blake to be with her for backup.

But if she took a chance and met face-to-face with Rocky, she might bring a swift and positive end to her investigation. As Hugh's accountant, Tim Rockwell had access to all the financial paperwork that could prove extortion and fraud. Before he abruptly quit six months ago, she'd found him in Hugh's home office at the mansion, a place he seldom went to work. She'd slipped into the large room on the first floor. After checking to make sure none of the security guards were around, she had closed the door and greeted Rocky. "Good afternoon, I'm surprised to see you here."

"There are a few records I needed to access for tax purposes." He'd stood behind the massive piece of carved, antique furniture that suited Hugh's large frame very well. In contrast, Rocky seemed dwarfed by the monstrous desk. "I'll be done in a minute."

"Take all the time you want," she'd said as she sauntered across the large, well-lit room with a wall of arched, multi-paned windows. "It's nice to see somebody who isn't carrying a gun or pushing a political agenda. I've always thought we had a lot in common, you and I."

She hadn't been lying. With her penchant for making agendas and plans, Jordan had accepted that she

was kind of a perfectionist who liked having everything organized.

"I think so, too." When Rocky smiled, he revealed
two prominent buckteeth that reinforced his nickname.
His dark eyes—magnified by round glasses—made
him look even more like a squirrel. "I can tell that you
like details. So do I. And you're very careful with your
money, aren't you?"

She and Rocky had had this discussion before. For
years, he'd wanted to combine her private savings, investments and accounts with the Waltham estate. Thank
goodness, she hadn't listened to his advice. "I won't
change my mind, not until I have unfettered access to
everything Hugh owns. We both know that's not going
to happen."

"Afraid not."

"I like doing my own accounting. It's a grown-up
activity, and I sometimes need a break from the kids."
She lowered herself into a chair on the opposite side of
the desk and gestured for him to sit. With a welcoming
smile, she hoped to get him talking. "You handle all
the payments for the house staff and nannies, right?"

"I do."

"Did we ever have a young woman named Bianca
working here?"

"Oh my, no." His nose twitched, and he blinked nervously. "Are you talking about the Bianca who was
murdered?"

She didn't try to hide her interest. Rocky would see
through a ruse. "I want to write an article about her
death. You know I'm a journalist. Can you help me?"

"I knew her. A beautiful girl with long black hair. She was so young. A tragic murder."

Jordan bit her lip to keep from debating the idea that the death of a pretty girl was more important than the demise of one who wasn't so lovely. She strongly believed all murder was heinous but didn't need the distraction. Reading Rocky's sad eyes told her that he'd known Bianca and mourned her. Maybe he knew who killed her. "Did you ever talk to her?"

"I heard her singing a lullaby in Spanish. I speak the language fluently, you know. Bianca confided in me, told me she was pregnant. Couldn't believe it, I just couldn't. She was so very young."

"So young." She leaned forward, resting her forearms on the desktop. "Did she speak of the father?"

"The father of her child? Why, yes. Yes, she did. She had fallen in love with him. He was older, a powerful man."

"You didn't approve," she said, encouraging him to keep talking.

"Of course not. He had obviously taken advantage of that sweet, young lady."

The name, tell me his name. She had been on the verge of an important discovery. Before she could push her advantage, the door to the office swung open and Ray Gruber stalked inside.

He snapped at her. "You don't belong here, Jordan."

"Well, maybe I don't live here anymore but it's still my house, Gruber. I can go anywhere I want."

"Don't play dumb. Move it."

She stood opposite Rocky at the desk and grinned at him. "I enjoyed our chat. I hope we can talk again soon."

They never had a chance. Less than a week later, Rocky had quit, causing her to wonder if their conversation had played a part in his disappearance.

She stared through the windshield and made a U-turn back toward the cabin. If she could talk to Rocky again—in person—he might tell her who was the father of Bianca's babies and who had murdered her. But she wouldn't take that risk until Blake could return with her. For once, she would exercise caution.

Chapter Fourteen

Blake had chosen his position carefully. Halfway up a craggy slope, he sat on an outcropping of red stone with his legs dangling. From there, he could see the kids at the lake and the driveway that led to the garage behind his cabin. Jordan was running late, only ten minutes, not enough for him to be seriously worried, but he couldn't help the stabbing anxiety that got worse as the seconds ticked slowly. The same foreboding had infected him at the airfield in Las Vegas. Jordan tended to get into trouble when she took off on her own. No matter how much she wanted to talk to Rocky, he needed for her to be careful, to curb her impulses and think ahead. More than anything, he wanted to pull her out of this risky investigation and establish a new normal for her and the twins—a normalcy that included him.

When he turned his head to the right, he had a view of Paddington Lake where the boys, wearing orange life jackets, zoomed across the glassy surface of the water in a motorboat owned by Chester Prynne. Blake had wanted to teach them how to handle a rowboat, in keeping with his old-fashioned-but-still-cool way of doing things, but when Chester glided up to the dock with the little red motorboat, the twins went wild. They loved going fast, and Blake didn't blame them. He often felt the need for speed.

Rotating his perspective, he looked back at the cabin. *Where the hell was she?* Earlier, when they talked about her shopping trip, he'd pointed out the advantages of going to the closest stores. There was nothing to be gained by driving to Aspen. Shopping would cost more, parking was a drag and she was more likely to run into wealthy people she knew from Arizona in the resort town.

Yelling from the twins drew his attention to the lake where Chester had allowed Alex to take over the steering. The small boy behind the wheel let out a squeal—so loud that he could be heard over the boat's motor—as he swooped from left to right. As far as Blake could tell, there was nobody else on the lake. The temperature had dropped to a chill that made it uncomfortable to drop a fishing line into the water and sit, waiting for a bite—somewhat like his current predicament. He couldn't force Jordan to be cautious. Nothing to do but wait patiently.

When Cooper took his turn and proved to be no less reckless than his brother, Blake silently cheered him on. *Attaboy!* Cooper tended to be more thoughtful and analytical, like his mom. It was good to see him acting like a kid.

When Blake spotted the Suburban, he stood on his outcropping and waved to Jordan with both arms, attracting her attention. She passed the turn onto the driveway, drove up the road below where he was standing, pulled over to the shoulder and parked. As he climbed down from the rock, she ran to meet him. "What's wrong? Where are the kids?"

"It's all good," he said. "Did you get your shopping taken care of?"

The roar of the motorboat on the lake drew her attention. She turned and stared. Her breath caught in her throat. "Is that my son driving the boat?"

"I think it's Cooper."

"Oh my God." She charged toward the dock. "How could you let them do that?"

"Stop." He caught her arm. "Chester is in the boat with them. They're wearing life jackets. And they're fine."

"How cold is that water? It looks freezing, and I want them out of there." She pulled away from him. "This is not your call, Blake."

Her attitude surprised him. Jordan never hesitated to take a risk with her own safety. She didn't needlessly put her twins in harm's way, but she'd literally stolen the boys away in the middle of the night and dragged them across the country. "I never thought you were one of those helicopter moms."

"What?"

"Isn't that what you call it when a parent hovers over their children, watching every move and being over-protective?"

"It is," she said. "And I'm not. At least, I never thought I was."

"Don't stop your kids from having fun."

At that moment, Chester took control of the boat and circled toward the dock. Both boys waved. She weakly lifted her hand and forced a smile. "I don't want to hover, but I worry about them, especially now. I keep thinking I've made a terrible mistake, and they're going to get hurt."

He slung an arm around her shoulder and gave her a hug. Though not a parent, he understood the delicate balance between protecting your loved ones and giving them enough freedom to make their own choices. Moments ago, he'd been worried that she intended to rush into Aspen on her own and confront her witness. But here she was. And everything was fine. At least, he hoped so.

In a carefully nonjudgmental voice, he asked, "Where did you shop?"

"Are you asking me if I drove to Aspen and tracked down Rocky the Flying Squirrel?"

"I was trying not to ask," he said.

"I thought about it," she admitted. "Earlier this year, before he disappeared, I had a talk with him. He knew about Bianca's pregnancy and might be able to name the father. If I could get a couple of minutes alone with him, I'm sure he'd tell me."

Bad idea. He wasn't in favor. "Approaching him would be a risk. You'd give away your location. You can't trust Rocky to be on your side."

"Frustrating." Gazing down at the dock, she leaned her back against his chest. The jasmine scent of her shampoo tickled his nose. "I'm running in place, not making headway."

He wrapped her in his embrace. "Did I mention that Chester is here?"

Blake tried not to make it sound like his old friend and mentor had flown across the lake to rescue the

twins from boredom like a superhero with his cape
flapping in the wind, but he couldn't help feeling that
Chester had the all the answers, including the solution
to her stuck investigation. Over the years, he'd made a
lot of friends, ranging from the President of the United
States to the guy with the waist-length beard who was
responsible for running the snowplow on the roads in
their area. Chester firmly believed that if you asked the
right person, you could accomplish anything.

When Blake had given him an outline of Jordan's
suspicions, he came up with the name of a high-ranking
official in the FBI, someone trustworthy to take over the
official investigation and hand it off to a federal prosecutor who would like nothing more than to take down
a sleazy political consultant who was using his position
for corruption. They'd relieve Jordan of all responsibility and take her out of danger.

Chester hiked up the slope behind the boys, who
had already moored the motorboat and stowed their life
jackets. Without even trying, the seventy-plus former
marine looked wise, determined and honorable. His
weathered features under his thick crest of white hair
were chiseled by time and experience. His athletic gait
matched his ramrod straight posture. *Semper Fi.* He
embodied the finest traits of the Corps. Surely, Jordan
would listen to him.

Cooper reached her first and flung his arms around
her middle while he looked up at her, reading the nu-
ance of her expression. "Did you see me, Mom? I drove
the boat. All by myself."

"Were you scared?" she asked.

"A little bit."

Her lips pinched together, then relaxed as she swallowed her reprimand. Instead, she focused on the positive. "Good for you, Coop. You overcame your fear but were still careful. And had fun."

"So much fun."

"I wasn't scared at all," Alex said as he grabbed her opposite side. "I think maybe I'll be a ship's captain instead of a helicopter pilot."

"Or you could be both," she said.

Now that they had their mother's approval, the kids turned to Blake, telling him how it felt to go really fast with the wind blowing and the water splashing and the fish jumping. "Better than any old rowboat," Alex said.

"Don't be so sure," Chester said. "Did you ever hear of being up the creek without a paddle? I'm telling you, kids, motorboats can run out of gas. Then you're stranded."

When he greeted Jordan, she gave him a hug and a kiss on the cheek, then said, "Thanks for watching over these little monkeys."

"Great kids." He beamed. "Any time you want to leave me in charge, I'm up for that duty."

She reflected his grin. "I fully intend to cash in on that offer."

"That's the idea," he said. "From what Blake told me, you've got enough on your plate."

AFTER THEY RETURNED to the cabin and had dinner, Jordan sent the boys upstairs to put away their new winter clothes, play with a sketching and tracing notebook and check out their brand-new snowshoes, which left tracks like monsters. After they rushed up the staircase, she refilled the coffee mugs and set out a plate of macadamia nut cookies Blake had picked up that morning from a bakery in Glenwood.

"How much did Blake tell you?" she asked Chester.

"I'll break it into three parts," he said. "First, he told me how your ex-husband—a real bastard—assaulted you and incarcerated you in an institution. The proof is your direct testimony."

"And the reason I won't be believed is counter-testimony from Hugh and from Dr. Merchant at the Institute who claims that I'm a danger to myself and others."

"Second," Chester said, "you've compiled a stack of evidence—paperwork and witness testimony—accusing your ex-husband of fraud, extortion, smuggling and money laundering. All this makes me wonder why you haven't contacted law enforcement."

"Hugh is a powerful man with far-reaching influence. Every time I put out feelers with district attorneys and police, my investigation was shut down. I want to be sure—one hundred percent sure—that Hugh will be tried and convicted."

"You've done remarkable work for a person who doesn't have the authority to compel cooperation from witnesses."

"She's good at convincing people to help her," Blake put in.

She had to agree. "My best witness is Tim Rockwell, my ex-husband's former accountant, who now lives in Aspen. I don't know if he'll talk to the authorities or not."

"If he's offered a deal, he'll talk," Chester said.

"Blake can verify this truth. When the bad guys get in trouble, they all talk."

"I hope you're right." If Chester Prynne could lift this responsibility from her shoulders, she'd be happy. Of course, she liked doing her own research and investigating, but these issues had grown exponentially too large for her to handle.

"Moving on to the third issue: the murder of Bianca Hernandez. You believe the ME withheld important evidence about the murder weapon and the DNA of her unborn twins. Additionally, the Flagstaff PD did a poor job of investigating this case."

"Correct." She appreciated his succinct analysis. "What do you think, Chester? Can you help me?"

"I'm retired." He reached for another cookie. This elderly gentleman had one of those metabolisms that allowed him to eat whatever he wanted and stay as lean as a whippet. Blake had the same ability. Maybe it was a military thing.

He continued. "I was never actually in law enforcement, but I worked with a number of federal officers when I was a marine."

"A full bird colonel," Blake said. "You can't get much higher."

She leaned back in her chair and sipped her coffee. "Chester, are you talking about the FBI? DEA? ICE? Any other acronym?"

"All of the above," he said. "I suggest we coordinate the investigation through a supervisory special agent for the FBI based in Denver, SSA Ferris Taggart."

"Taggart has an excellent reputation." Though impressed that Chester knew this guy, she didn't quite believe that such a high-ranking, important fed would be interested in her complicated issue. "Why would he get involved?"

"Why wouldn't he?" Chester sat up straight, took a bite of cookie and chewed. "According to your evidence, your ex-husband has broken dozens of laws, including murder. It's the duty of the FBI to check him out. Not only will Taggart organize the gathering of further information and scare the pants off those idiots in Flagstaff who concealed evidence, he can install you and the twins in a safe house."

Relief washed over her like a gentle, warm wave, soothing her tense muscles and relaxing her choke hold on self-restraint. The stress had been extreme, nearly unbearable. She'd hardly dared to admit how frightened she'd been for the kids. If her actions had inadvertently put them in danger, she'd never forgive herself. A safe house sounded like a decent solution.

For the twins…but not for her.

Jordan wasn't ready to give up. Months of her life had been invested in sifting through investment documents in her ex-husband's office, snapping photos of dangerous people who came though their mansion with payoffs for Hugh and tracking down the household workers, like Bianca and her sister, who had been forced into unpaid labor. Working with Spike, she reviewed reams of computer records from the casinos—including the Magic Lamp—that had performed money-laundering operations.

"When can I meet with SSA Taggart?" she asked.

Chester took his cell phone from the pocket of his

fishing vest and held it aloft like the Statue of Liberty's beacon. "I'll call him now."

"It's not too late?"

"Only seven o'clock. He'll be awake."

With a heartfelt smile, she said, "Thank you."

While Chester left the table and sauntered into Blake's office, she drained her coffee mug and looked over at the man who sat beside her. Though she had dozens of valuable contacts, including Hornsby, a former news anchor, and Spike, the computer genius who helped her pursue her investigation, Blake's friend held the key to concluding her ex-husband's crime spree.

She leaned close and whispered in his ear. "And thank you, too. I couldn't have done this without you."

"You would have found a way," he said. "Like I said before, when you're on the trail of an investigation, you're a pit bull."

"Those dogs are fierce." She stroked his cheek, feeling the stubble that had grown over the past few days. The more she relaxed, the more she was able to express the attraction she felt. "Pit bulls also have the reputation of being extremely loyal and affectionate."

"Like you." He caught hold of her hand, held it to his lips and ran a trail of kisses down her index finger to her thumb. "Fierce but loyal."

"If you were a dog…"

"Let's not go there," he said. "I'm not interested in being another species."

Nor was she. Being this close to him awakened the womanly urges she hadn't allowed herself to feel for years. "Great Dane. Because you have a smooth coat. You're big and strong and very handsome."

"Tell me more," he murmured.

"Let's not start something we can't finish." She glanced toward the closed door to the office. "Chester is going to rejoin us at any moment."

"We've been apart for too long. I've missed you."

She felt the same. She missed the sound of his voice, the look in his eyes, his taste, his scent. So often, she'd thought of the little kisses, hugs and touches that led, more often than not, to passion. More than that, she savored their companionship. He always seemed to know what she was thinking. Not that their relationship had been all about lust. He supported her needs and desires. He could always make her laugh.

Through the years, even after she married Hugh, her abiding fondness for Blake had comforted her. In moments of great joy, she had longed to share her heart with him…like the day when the twins were born. She'd been in the delivery room alone because Congress was in session and Hugh—even though he wasn't an elected senator—didn't want to miss anything. At least, that was what he'd told her. And she'd been so wrapped up in the impending birth that she didn't have the time or inclination to figure out if he was lying. When she held her tiny baby boys, she didn't think of Hugh. Instead, she saw Blake's dimpled smile and heard his voice telling her that she'd done a good job. She'd imagined his kiss on her forehead. With a sigh, she returned to the present. "I'm glad we're finally together."

Before she could show him how much closer she wanted to be, Chester returned to the table. He sat and gave a quick nod. "Taggart wants to see you as soon as possible."

"Yes!" She raised both fists in victory.

"I have a helicopter pad at my ranch on the other side of the lake," Chester said. "SSA Taggart and a couple of his top agents will be here tomorrow, if we don't get hit by a major snowstorm."

Tomorrow? That meant she still had tonight to make a difference. "Chester, can you stay with the kids for a couple of hours?"

"Sure," he said. "What do you have in mind?"

She glanced toward Blake. "I want to take one last run at Rocky in Aspen. Will you come with me?"

"Oh, hell yes. You're not going alone." He rose to his feet, towering over the table like Thor. In that one move, he asserted his physical dominance. "I'll drive."

She didn't need to ask who he thought was in charge. In his mind, he would—for the most part—direct the mission. She decided not to interrupt his fantasy.

Chapter Fifteen

Buckled into the passenger seat of the Suburban, Jordan didn't tease herself into thinking that her current plan had much chance of success. The possibility of Rocky agreeing to talk to her was minimal, and she promised Blake that she wouldn't force the issue.

"Here's what I want to do," she said. "We'll park outside his multi-million-dollar mountain chalet, and I'll make a phone call to him on Spike's encrypted phone. Rocky won't know where I am, and I'll be careful not to give away my location."

"Don't expect a chalet," he warned her. "Millions in Aspen doesn't guarantee a mansion. I don't know the exact location of this address, but the area is known for simple houses on multi-acre lots. Your squirrel is paying for privacy."

"Makes sense." Tim Rockwell wasn't the type of person to hire a bunch of security guys to protect him. "We should assume he has sophisticated camera surveillance."

Blake nodded. "Why is it necessary for us to drive to his house if all you're going to do is make a phone call?"

"He might invite me to come inside."

"Doubtful."

"And if he runs, we can follow him."

"I'm not loving this strategy, but I guess it can't hurt."

Even if he was merely humoring her, she appreciated his presence. Gazing through the windshield at the night sky where ragged wisps of clouds obscured the waning moon, she snuggled into the heated bucket seat and exhaled a sigh. "What do you love, Blake?"

"What?"

"You said you don't love my plan. So, tell me, what do you love?"

He took a long pause before answering, and she studied his strong profile, which was outlined by the dashboard lights. Sometimes, she forgot how handsome he was with his high forehead perfectly balanced with a rugged jaw. His deep-set eyes, which were a brilliant blue in the sunlight, stared straight ahead. She knew he was thinking, choosing his words with care.

"This," he said.

Jordan had hoped for more. "Could you be a teensy-tiny bit more specific?"

"Right now, in this moment, I'm almost perfectly happy. We're on a mission. Together. I love the sense of purpose, even though your plan isn't great."

Oddly, she knew what he meant. They'd never been a couple who were content to sit quietly in front of a crackling fireplace with nothing to do. "What else?"

"I love being in Colorado, cruising along a mountain road with the night shadows playing hide-and-seek across the faces of hills and depths of valleys. The crisp taste of snow in the air pleases me. Also, I love knowing the boys are safe at home with Chester watching over them."

So far, his words reflected a near match for her own feelings, except in one particular arena. He'd mentioned how he liked her as a companion, a teammate working toward a goal. But he hadn't spoken about his feelings for her as a woman, hadn't mentioned an attraction to her or complimented the way she looked. Though it seemed silly to worry about such superficial things, she wanted to know. They'd been together 24/7 since Saturday night, and it was Monday evening. They'd shared a few kisses, hugs and touches but nothing approaching intimacy. She wanted to know…if he wanted her…as much as she wanted him.

In a quiet, humble voice—not her style at all—she asked, "How do you feel about me?"

"Are you asking if I love you?"

"Of course not." She scoffed. "I'd never put you on the spot like that."

"Good, because there's no way I'd risk an answer to that question. Too dangerous."

"Don't tell me that a big, strong marine is scared of falling in love."

He pantomimed zipping his lips and throwing away the key before he said, "The forecasters are predicting heavy snowfall tomorrow."

"What are you talking about?"

"When in doubt, talk about the weather. Or sports. How about those Broncos?"

Her question wasn't really answered, but his admitted nervousness gave her reassurance. When he thought of her in that special way, he lapsed into tongue-tied panic. *Good.* "Actually, I wouldn't mind hearing how the Broncos are doing."

"Three wins, two losses. They play Kansas City on Sunday."

"Really." Her eyes narrowed. "I haven't seen you reading a newspaper or noticed you listening to sports radio, and we don't have easy access to internet. How do you know the team standings?"

"True sports fans have chips implanted in their brains that constantly spew out stats and details about their favorite teams." He glanced toward her and raised his eyebrows. "Speaking of chips, didn't you tell me that Spike was going to hook us up with some kind of mysterious, black-market computer connection that couldn't be traced?"

She dug into her beat-up, leather messenger bag and pulled out a tablet with a ten-inch screen that she generally used for reading mystery novels. "I'm hoping he can do that tonight."

"What are you going to do with the tablet?"

"Rocky has always been kind of a computer geek. I'll bet he has surveillance cameras and maybe even hidden microphones around his house. Spike might be able to hack into his system, giving us a view of what's happening inside his modest multi-million-dollar home."

"I like it. Good way to gather data without putting ourselves in danger."

Barely consulting the GPS, Blake confidently made all the turns until he was driving along Highway 82, which followed the flow of the Roaring Fork River. Clearly, he'd taken this route before. Suspicious, she asked, "How do you know where you're going?"

"I come up here to ski. I tried snowboarding a couple of times but didn't like it as much. Nothing beats swooping downhill, flying over moguls. Maybe you can come with me on my next run."

If she stayed in Colorado, she'd like nothing better than to ski with him. But there was no point in making future plans. She might be on the run again, might be sequestered in an FBI safe house or locked away in prison, charged with kidnapping. Shaking her head, she tried to shove those dire, depressing possibilities from her mind.

As a woman who liked to have things organized, she hated not having a clue about what her future would be. How could she consider a relationship with Blake when tomorrow might bring unforeseen complications? She had to rely on other skills—abilities she'd developed as an investigative reporter. She'd dig for all the information she could find while keeping an open mind. Most of all, she'd stop worrying about things she couldn't control.

"The twins," she said in a clear voice that didn't betray her tension, "they should learn how to ski."

"Kids catch on fast. When they fall in the snow, they don't have far to go before they hit the ground. Your boys will be racing down the slopes in no time."

"You didn't grow up in Colorado." She remembered a long-ago conversation about their early lives. "It was somewhere in Illinois."

"Peoria," he said. "I went to college at Texas A&M on a football scholarship. Go Aggies. That was when I started scheduling my vacations for Colorado, and I met Chester. Whenever possible, I'd stay with him."

"And ski."

"He was my surrogate dad, newly retired with plenty of time to take me on as a project, especially after I tore my ACL and couldn't play football."

He was lucky to have found a strong male role model to replace the father who had abandoned his family. "If you hadn't met Chester, what do you think you'd be doing?"

"Maybe I would have become a teacher." He glanced toward her. "And you? Did you ever consider a career other than journalism?"

"Not that I remember, but I didn't do a lot of heavy thinking. Like Alex, I thought I'd take on all kinds of different occupations. Then I realized that, as a journalist, I could pretend to be all those things and more." She shrugged. "One thing I never imagined was being a mother."

Reminiscing and just talking with him felt comfortable and pleasant. She leaned back in her seat and stared out at the night landscape as they rolled along the highway toward Aspen, coming closer to her witness, the squirrel who might bring a satisfying conclusion to her investigation. If only she could get him to talk to the FBI, Rocky would provide reams of evidence about her ex-husband's fraud, larceny and money laundering.

Blake exited the highway and drove into an area known as Cougar Gulch. He quickly assured her that the cougars weren't all sexy, wealthy, older women who preyed on handsome, young ski bums. "The area is named for real mountain lions."

"I'm sure you didn't come down this twisty road to

go skiing," she said. "Are we headed in the right direction?"

"I dated a woman who lived around here."

"Your own private cougar?"

"Not that it's any of your business, but we were the same age. She flew jets in the navy."

Jordan was immediately interested. "Is she one of those pilots who take off from aircraft carriers? I'd love to talk to her. Can you set up a meeting?"

"A meeting with two of my former girlfriends? Hmm, let me think about it." He shook his head and mumbled something that sounded like a negative. Then he switched topics. "Hey, I heard the temperature would drop twenty degrees in two hours tomorrow afternoon."

When in doubt, talk about the weather... At a stop sign, she craned her neck to read a street sign. As he'd suggested, the houses were smaller than mansion-sized and set far apart on large, wooded lots. "We're getting closer."

"It's just over the next hill," he said, checking the GPS. "I'm going to drive past. We can check the place out and then find a vantage point to observe Rocky's nest."

As they cruised down the street, she peered through her window at a long, paved driveway leading to a two-story home with an impressive entry facade of chiseled granite blocks. Cedar planks alternated with several picture windows to form the other walls and a large deck. On one side a granite rock formation echoed the entryway architecture. A grove of aspen separated the house from its neighbors to the north. Though there was a three-car garage, two vehicles parked at the front door—a black SUV and a dark sedan—both had tinted windows.

"Looks like he has guests." She checked her wristwatch. "It's 9:47 p.m."

"A dinner party?"

"Not Rocky. He's not a guy who does a lot of socializing."

"Aspen might have changed him. Does he have a girlfriend?"

"I don't know." She'd never bothered to ask, which was a lapse in judgment on her part. When researching a subject, she usually gathered as much info as possible, starting with the most important people in their lives.

Blake circled through the streets of Cougar Gulch, passing wide-spaced houses and artistically placed trees and shrubs until he found an overlook above Rocky's granite-and-cedar house where he parked at the curb. From her window, Jordan peered through a thicket of pine trees. She could see the driveway and the front door. The place looked innocent with light glowing from the picture windows. She narrowed her gaze. *Who was visiting Rocky?*

"In the glove box," Blake said, "there's a pair of night-vision binoculars."

"You're brilliant." She popped the latch and took out the lenses, which were easily adjusted and clarified the view. "There's nothing going on. You'd think with all those windows, few of which have curtains, that I could see somebody walking around."

He reached into the back seat and grabbed the handle on a gym bag. "I brought other supplies. Flashlights, a burner phone, granola bars, bottled water and anything else we might need for a stakeout."

Being on a stakeout conjured up visions of dark, dirty streets and seedy neighborhoods. Instead they were parked in a lavishly landscaped area with incredibly expensive homes, a clear reminder that wealthy people—like her ex-husband—also committed crimes.

"Do you have your Glock?" she asked, still staring through the binoculars.

"Yes."

"Did you bring a weapon for me?"

"There's no need," he said resolutely. "You aren't going to be confronting anybody."

Though she didn't like the restriction, she knew he was correct. She didn't worry about her own safety, but if she revealed her presence to the wrong people, the twins would be in danger. "I'll be careful," she promised, "but I want to get out of the car and find a better spot for watching."

"Wait." He reached up and disabled the light that came on when the car door opened.

"Smart. We don't need to attract attention."

"Go. I'm right behind you," he said. "If I tap your shoulder, stop."

"Why?"

"We need to avoid sight lines from Rocky's house that might pick up our movements. Trust me on this. I know how to evade enemy detection on an approach."

She darted between the trees and carefully moved to a different angle. Fallen needles and pine cones crunched underfoot, not too loudly, but enough to scare away the critters. A chilly breeze spun through the tree trunks and brushed her cheeks. She pulled up the hood on her purple puffer jacket and dug into the pocket for knitted gloves. Following close behind her, Blake might have been nearly invisible—in his black parka and black watch cap with a smudged "N" for *navy*—if he hadn't been such a large man.

After poking around in the landscaped forest, she found a hiding place behind a thicket and a boulder where they had a clear view of Rocky's house. She still hadn't spotted anyone moving around inside. She leaned against the large, warm body beside her.

"If something happens, what should we do?" she whispered.

"We can't arrest them. We're not cops. And we don't have backup." His low, stakeout-level voice caressed her. "Maybe record it on your cell phone."

She'd almost forgotten her super-encrypted phone. Now would be a great time for Spike to hack into Rocky's surveillance system. She pulled off her gloves to text him. Before the screen flared into light, Blake opened his parka and made her a warm tent where she could hide the cell phone. As she sent her text, she realized that it wouldn't be necessary for them to do a physical stakeout if Spike could access cameras inside the house.

She had just received a return text from Spike, telling her that he could manage the hack but it would take a while, when Blake whispered.

"Something's happening," he said.

With her cell phone dark, she emerged and raised her night-vision binoculars to her eyes. The front door had opened. A heavyset man came onto the porch. Twice as big as Rocky, who scampered beside him, the giant threw both arms wide to embrace the night and turned his big, round face up to the skies. There was no mistaking his identity.

It was Caspar Khaled.

Jordan covered her mouth to hide her gasp of surprise. Two other men with parkas emerged from the house, and she recognized casino bosses who had chased her down Fremont Street in Las Vegas. Spike had told her that Khaled took off in a private jet. Apparently, this was his destination.

A simple explanation for his visit might be that Rocky worked for him. Possibly, Khaled's connection with the accountant had nothing to do with her ex-husband's many crimes. But she doubted the casino owner's innocence. Her visit must have alerted him to potential issues with the money-laundering scheme, and he came here to make sure Rocky didn't implicate him.

Another man stepped outside. He covered his shaved head with a furry Russian hat. His sleek jacket was tailored leather, and he strutted as he descended the two stairs from the porch and went to the dark sedan. The sight of him fired her rage. Blood boiling, she glared daggers.

"Dr. Stephen Merchant."

His cruel diagnosis had kept her imprisoned in the Gateway Institute. At his direction, she'd been drugged and restrained. She'd suffered solitary confinement, electroconvulsive shock treatment and hours in a straitjacket. Merchant was worse than Gruber because, as a doctor, he ought to know better.

His presence at Rocky's house represented definitive evidence that Hugh was involved in this late-night meeting. In a sharp but quiet voice, she said, "I want to go down there."

"Let the FBI arrest them."

"They're too rich," she said. "They'll get away with their crimes."

"Not this time."

Together, she and Blake would take their vengeance. For Bianca. And for Abigail. And for all the people Hugh and his associates had hurt and swindled. When these monsters were locked away, she and her children would finally be safe.

Chapter Sixteen

"Don't worry," SSA Ferris Taggart said. "Jordan Reese-Waltham will not be charged with kidnapping. You have my word."

Though relieved, Blake had to ask, "Why not?"

"The story her ex-husband has been telling is that she's taken the twins for a short vacation, and I'm choosing to believe she has his permission. My guess is that he wanted to avoid contact with the FBI or other law enforcement."

"Good guess."

Taggart and three other FBI agents had landed at the helipad on Chester's property less than an hour ago and commandeered the use of Chester's rugged Land Rover for their stay, leaving him with the Silverado. Their initial plan was to question Tim Rockwell, aka Rocky the Flying Squirrel, at his home in Aspen. Weather-wise, they'd been lucky. No snow, not yet, but the blue skies had already begun to fade as the storm over Ice Mountain came closer.

While Jordan and the kids stayed at his cabin, Blake had driven the Suburban to Chester's property for the meeting. The two old warriors, Chester and Taggart, had greeted each other with an exchange of salutes and hugs. Both tall and lean, they resembled each other in other ways as well. They both had white hair, neatly trimmed, and no facial hair. Taggart's most prominent feature was his thick, gray eyebrows, which pulled into a scowl when they got down to business.

Jordan had sent the fat flamingo flash drive with the evidence she'd gathered to use against Hugh along with a packet of photos and witness interviews. Her explanation of the data might have been clearer than Blake's would be, but she preferred to have Blake make the first contact. Some of her research involved somewhat illegal methods, especially when using Spike's cybertalents.

Before Blake left the cabin, she made him promise not to reveal Spike's unauthorized hack of the surveillance cameras at Rocky's house. Using her tablet, she could see the front and back doors to his house as well as the interior entry and his office, where they'd watched him open a wall safe hidden behind a painting of Mount Sopris.

"I'm looking forward to meeting her," Taggart said.

Blake shot him a suspicious look. "But not to arrest her, right?"

"The opposite," Taggart said. "I want to recruit her. She'd make an outstanding agent. Did you see the video posted on YouTube by a tourist at the Magic Lamp?"

"No, I haven't." A headache thrummed against his forehead. When she'd ventured into Las Vegas, he hadn't been thrilled about the plan. Now that they'd seen Khaled at Rocky's, he disliked it even more.

Taggart summoned one of the other agents and asked for his phone. After thumbing through the memory, he held up the video for Blake to see. "Check it out. Using her titanium baton, she takes down three guys, including Khaled, who's a giant."

On the screen, he saw Jordan evading shirtless men in harem pants with kendo moves and Filipino martial arts. She was fast, graceful and dangerous. While Blake still didn't approve of the risk she'd taken, he couldn't help being proud of her.

"Amazing," Taggart said. "Where did she learn how to do that?"

"I taught her."

"And I'd try to recruit you if Chester hadn't already told me that you're a marine to your core." He stalked toward the Land Rover. "Let's head out. I want to beat the snow."

Before he left, Blake spoke to Chester and asked him to return to the cabin with the Suburban. "I don't expect trouble, but I'd feel better if you were there with Jordan and the kids."

"Don't worry." Chester echoed the advice from Taggart. "This is going to turn out okay."

Blake wished he could be that certain.

Jordan couldn't avoid having this conversation any longer. The twins had cooperated in every way that was truly important. With little encouragement, they'd accepted her directions, ranging from boarding a helicopter to not drinking coffee. She owed them explanations for why she'd torn them away from their bedroom in the middle of the night, why they hadn't been able to say goodbye to their father and why they had to keep running.

After they lit a fire on the hearth in the front room of the cabin, she seated them on the plaid sofa. Alex sat on her left, and Cooper on the right. She wrapped her arms around them. As best she could, Jordan vowed to tell them the truth. Snuggling them close, she dropped kisses on the tops of their heads. "Everything I've done, every decision I've made comes from love."

"What are you talking about?" Cooper asked. "What decisions?"

"I had good reasons for taking you away from your dad." No way could she explain the complicated crimes Hugh had committed. Nor would she mention the terrible murder of Bianca. Not wanting to irreparably poison their relationship with their father, she wouldn't talk about the violence he'd done to her. "The important thing is this. Your dad still loves you. And I love you. None of this is your fault."

"Okay," Alex said. "Can we go outside? I want to put on my snowshoes."

"But there's no snow. Not yet."

Cooper said, "We ought to go down to the lake and check on Chester's boat. He left it here."

"I want you to know," she said, "that things might get dangerous."

Alex rose up on his knees, put his arms around her neck and kissed her cheek. "It's okay, Mom. We'll take care of you."

"You told us this stuff before," Cooper said. "When we moved into the little blue house with the tire swing. I liked that place."

That talk had taken place over a year ago when they were four, and it surprised her that Cooper remembered. He was so much older and wiser than his chronological age. "Here's what's different about this time. Chester and Blake talked to a friend of theirs. His name is Ferris Taggart. He's an FBI agent, and he's going to help us."

"FBI?" Alex's eyes opened as wide as saucers. "An FBI agent. Cool."

"The thing to remember is that he's a good guy." She looked from one twin to the other. "He might want you to stay at a safe house. Do you know what that is?"

Cooper guessed. "A house built out of steel that nobody can break into?"

"Or iron," Alex said. "Iron is stronger."

"It looks like a regular house, but a safe house is a supersecure location with surveillance and security. There will be other FBI agents to guard you and keep you protected. I know that sounds scary, but it might be necessary."

If Hugh or Gruber or even Dr. Merchant came after her, she didn't want the boys to be hurt by accident. Though she hoped that Hugh wouldn't endanger his sons, she couldn't be sure about him or the others. She continued, "If you have questions, ask me. I'll tell you the truth."

"I've got one." Cooper raised his hand as if he were in school. "Is Blake your boyfriend?"

In spite of herself, she grinned. "And what does that have to do with safe houses?"

"You promised to tell us the truth," Alex said. "Is he your lovey-dovey?"

"I like Blake."

"Are you going to marry him?" Cooper asked.

She gestured helplessly. "He hasn't asked me."

There was a knock at the front door. Chester called out, "Hey, you guys, let me in."

The boys dashed to answer. While Cooper punched in the code in the keypad, Alex waited for the lock to disengage and pulled the door open. He hugged Chester and said, "You're friends with an FBI guy."

"You betcha. He's a supervisory special agent."

"How come he's so special?"

Chester shrugged. "All the agents call themselves special. I don't know why."

Though Jordan felt like she'd lost control of her conversation with the twins, she hoped they'd gained some level of understanding. On the plus side, they didn't seem frightened at all.

She grinned at Chester. "Did you get all those special agents pointed in the right direction?"

"I did, and Blake went with them to Rocky's house."

She excused herself and went into the office to check on the computer feed Spike had arranged. Since Rocky's surveillance camera didn't have audio, she could only guess at what the tall, lean agent was holding up, probably a wallet with a badge. No doubt, he was saying something like, "Open up, we have a warrant."

Faced with three FBI agents and Blake, Rocky trembled. Behind his round glasses, his eyes blinked several times as though he could erase the sight of them. For him, the arrival of the feds meant the end of his life in crime. No more multi-million-dollar properties. No more hiding out in one of the most beautiful resorts in the world. No more freedom. The flying squirrel was losing his wings.

THOUGH ROCKY'S HOUSE wasn't as big as a mansion, Blake could tell that no money had been spared with the furnishings. Original paintings hung from the walls, and unique sculptures lurked in every corner. The real treasure couldn't be purchased at any price—the picture windows framed panoramic views of forests, rock formations and snow-covered mountains that were partially obscured by gray-blue storm clouds. A family of elk, including a buck with a full rack of antlers, drank from a creek and darted into the pine forest. A golden eagle soared overhead.

Though the two agents accompanying Taggart set out to search the house, Rocky tried to treat the appearance of the FBI as a social event. He went to the kitchen, made a fresh pot of coffee and put together a plate of sausage, crackers and cheeses, which he placed on the dining room table along with square appetizer plates.

"It's not quite lunchtime," Rocky said, "but you gentlemen must be hungry. Please help yourselves."

Apparently, Taggart decided to play along. He took the seat at the end of the table and gestured for Rocky to sit to his right. He put a slice of cheese onto a wheat cracker. "You're a busy man, Mr. Rockwell. You had guests last night."

"Caspar Khaled and some of his men stopped by." He grinned, showing off his prominent buckteeth and trying to look friendly. "I used to work for him."

"At the Magic Lamp in Las Vegas."

"A lovely casino on Fremont. Since I was based in Flagstaff, I didn't get to visit him often. Most of our business was online."

"You were his accountant."

"One of many."

"Did Hugh Waltham introduce you?"

"I believe so. My work with Khaled mostly involved advice on investment and taxes."

Unprompted, he launched into a discussion on how profit and loss had to balance each other out, and the unique issues faced by casinos. The more he talked, the calmer he became. His words worked like a pressure valve, alleviating the tension he had to be feeling.

Taggart interrupted the monologue. "You said you were Khaled's former accountant. How did your relationship end?"

"We're still friends. That's obvious. That's why he felt comfortable visiting me." He jumped to his feet. "I retired. That's why I don't work for him anymore."

"I'll need to see your records for the Magic Lamp," Taggart said. "Just to review the paperwork."

"Fine." Rocky spat the word. "Look all you want. You won't find anything wrong."

His attitude told Blake that Rocky either had a double set of books that wouldn't show the discrepancies of money laundering or the squirrel had great confidence in his abilities.

Taggart gave an easygoing smile and rubbed his clean-shaven chin as if remembering a beard. His thick eyebrows arched as he nodded. "You're correct, Mr. Rockwell."

"About what?"

"I won't find anything wrong when I look over your books. I'm not a numbers guy. But the forensic accountants at the FBI are among the best in the world at sighting discrepancies. If your digits don't line up exactly right, they'll figure it out."

The color faded from Rocky's face, and he sank into his chair.

Blake wished Jordan could be here. She was familiar with Rocky and all his ploys. Her knowledge might prove invaluable. Unfortunately, the hacked video feed from Rocky's surveillance cameras didn't include the dining area, which meant she wouldn't be able to see what they were doing.

He had an idea. Excusing himself from the conversation between Taggart and Rocky, he went to the office where the other two agents searched through file drawers. Blake waved to the camera, hoping that Jordan was watching. He borrowed a cell phone from one of the agents, held it up toward the camera and used it to call her super-encrypted number.

She answered, "What are you doing?"

"I'm putting you on mute but leaving this phone on. When I go into the other rooms, you'll be able to hear what we're talking about. So far, Rocky hasn't said anything we don't know, but he's nervous as hell."

"Thanks," she whispered. "Be careful."

He dropped the cell phone into a pocket in his fleece vest and returned to the dining table where Rocky sat, shoulders slumped. The squirrel looked like he was about to vomit.

Taggart continued, "Your other guest last night was Dr. Stephen Merchant. Did you do accounting work for him?"

"He's my doctor."

"Dr. Merchant is a psychiatrist."

"A while ago, I had a breakdown. Hugh arranged for me to be treated at Dr. Merchant's institute."

"When was that?" Blake asked.

Since he'd been mostly quiet, his question was unexpected. Taggart repeated it.

"About a year and a half ago," Rocky said.

Which was right around the time that Jordan had become aware of her ex-husband's crimes and started poking around. And when Hugh beefed up his security team.

Rocky pulled off his round glasses and swabbed away tears before they streaked down his cheeks. "Dr. Merchant saved my life. I'd do anything for him."

"What set off your breakdown?" Blake asked.

Glasses back on his nose, Rocky glared at him. "You're the boyfriend, aren't you? The guy Jordan used to be in love with."

"We're talking about you," Blake said. "What caused your breakdown?"

"No, no," Rocky said, "we're talking about you. You live nearby. On Ice Mountain. Near Chester Prynne. Is that where Jordan is hiding? Did she take her kids there?"

He could almost feel the cell phone in his pocket buzzing and imagined Jordan yelling at Rocky, telling him it was none of his business where she'd gone or who she'd been with.

"You don't get to ask questions," Taggart said. "It's your job to give me answers."

"Let's drop this charade," Rocky said as he straightened his spine and drew himself up to his full height, which couldn't have been more than five-six. "I have nothing more to say. It's time for me to call my lawyer."

"You'll need a criminal lawyer, somebody who knows how to work a jury."

"Oh, please. I might have fudged the numbers, but any crimes I may or may not have committed are minor, punishable by a fine. No big deal."

"Think again, Mr. Rockwell." Taggart glared while Rocky fidgeted. "I expect to charge you with murder."

A harsh sob pushed through the small man's lips. Then he whispered her name.

"Bianca."

Chapter Seventeen

At the cabin, Jordan listened, mesmerized, as Tim Rockwell reported that he had not seen the killers inflict those fatal injuries, stabbing and slashing. But he admitted that he witnessed the aftermath. Rocky had found the body.

In a park in Flagstaff not far from his home, he'd gone for an evening jog and noticed her, broken and bleeding, at the side of the asphalt path. In a ragged voice, he told them how he recognized her, remembered her beauty and her gentle smile. "I knew right away that she was dead. So much blood, so much. Her eyes were wide open, staring up at Heaven."

He'd made an anonymous call to the police, not wanting to get involved, and then he went back to his house and pulled down the shades.

His cowardice disgusted Jordan. Too frightened to sit with the body, he'd left Bianca alone and unattended in the night. A final insult.

Taggart pressured him for more details. "What time was it? Did you see anyone else? Why would Bianca be in that neighborhood? Who killed her?"

"I don't know." She imagined Rocky wringing his

small hands. "I didn't really know her, didn't know anything about her, except…"

"Tell me," Taggart insisted.

"She had a beautiful singing voice. Sweet as an angel."

"Where did you hear her singing?"

"Sometimes, she worked at the Flagstaff house as a kitchen helper. She wasn't on the regular payroll but filled in when necessary. Waltham throws a lot of dinner parties and needs extra staff to help out."

Taggart instructed him to repeat his testimony again and again. Each time, Rocky recalled more detail. He spoke of the scratchy chirp of crickets in the night and the strangely metallic smell of blood when he neared the body. On the fourth repetition, his description had expanded from a few sentences to a long, complicated story. Still, he swore that he hadn't seen the murderer.

Finding an actual witness to Bianca's killing represented a big leap forward in Jordan's investigation. She wished Rocky had taken pictures with his cell phone, especially when he described the body being blood-soaked and lying in the green, green grasses. Had Bianca been killed somewhere else and moved to the park? The police description of the crime scene had been too vague to draw meaningful conclusions, but the police couldn't ignore the similarity between the scars on her wrist and the medical examiner's photos of Bianca's wounds. She had new evidence. With the addition of Rocky's testimony, she could force the Flagstaff police to reopen the cold case.

Right now, she had something more urgent to worry about. Rocky had recognized Blake and knew about this cabin. If he knew, she suspected the others were aware of her supposedly safe hideaway. They needed to move. The time had come to tuck the kids away in a safe house.

After punching in the code to deactivate the alarm at the front door, she went outside and headed down to where Chester had taken the boys, to the edge of Paddington Lake. She saw them at the end of the dock, throwing pebbles at the water and watching the ripples spread.

Still holding the cell phone, she listened to Taggart and Blake questioning Rocky about his other clients. His employers, including B and W Employ as well as two smaller casinos, formed a web of connections with Hugh sitting at the center like a poisonous spider.

She waved to the kids and signaled for them to climb the hill. As soon as they got here, she'd herd them into the Suburban and drive to Chester's house. A prudent solution.

Over the cell phone, she heard a door slam. Someone else joined the group at Rocky's house. The voice of her ex-husband came through the cell phone and echoed through her memories like a nightmare.

"You must be Captain Blake Delaney," Hugh Waltham said. "Finally, we meet."

Blake sized him up. When he saw Hugh on TV, he thought the guy was good-looking. In person, he wasn't as polished. Hugh wore appropriate clothes for the mountains: boots, jeans and flannel shirt under a fishing vest with multiple pockets. Jordan's ex-husband appeared to be a confident, successful gentleman, but

Blake saw a monster who had ordered an attack on Jordan and had locked her away at the Institute. Hugh's velvety, politician's voice oozed with treachery, ready to lie at the slightest provocation. Though he wore expensive aftershave, a rank smell emanated from him. Their handshake reminded Blake of the scaly appendage of a lizard.

Blake turned his back and distanced himself.

Taggart presented himself in a more civil manner. "What brings you to Colorado?"

"I'm here to visit my old pal, Rocky."

Blake saw terror in the small man's eyes. Though Rocky tried to smile, his mouth trembled. All his self-control focused on a simple question. "Would you like coffee?"

"You bet." Hugh sat at the table and leaned back in his chair. "Well, gentlemen, what are we talking about?"

"Murder," Blake said.

Hugh bobbed his head, and his carefully barbered blond hair skimmed across his tanned forehead. Everything about him showed a careful, camera-ready polish, from his buffed fingernails to his perfect teeth. His eyes were a swampy green instead of bright blue like Jordan and the twins. He gave a condescending chuckle. "Murder, eh? That's a big issue. You like to jump right in, don't you?"

"I don't waste time," Blake said.

"And so, Captain Delaney, who do you think Rocky killed?"

"Not funny." The small man darted back into the room with a fresh mug of coffee for his former employer. Wielding a glass carafe, he refilled for the others. "Please help yourselves to cheese and sausage."

"Charcuterie," Hugh said. "One of my favorite snacks."

"I know," Rocky said.

Blake wondered if he'd been expecting Hugh to drop by or if he kept stocked up on sausage and cheese just in case. The tension around the table was enough to give anybody indigestion, but Hugh and Taggart continued to fill their square appetizer plates with cheese, crackers and sausage, as if to show they weren't disturbed.

"The victim's name," Taggart said, "was Bianca Hernandez."

"Oh, yeah, I remember." Hugh stacked Swiss cheese on top of something that looked like pepperoni but was probably ten times more expensive. "It was a while ago. Did she work for me, Rocky?"

"I believe she did. In the kitchen."

Blake much preferred Rocky's earlier angst and nervousness. The more casual attitude offended him. Bianca deserved better. "She was sixteen years old and pregnant with twins."

"Tragic," Hugh said. "But I don't know what this has to do with Rocky. Or me."

"The killer was never arrested. The murder became another cold case, tucked away in the depths of the police archives," Taggart explained, with a bitterness that made Blake think he'd been in this position before. "The initial police investigation was sloppy, with questionable handling of DNA. And—surprise, surprise— we have new evidence."

"Good for you," Hugh said as he reached for a fat, red, smoked chorizo sausage. "I'm surprised the FBI has time to check on local police matters. What am I missing? Is a serial killer involved or another murder?"

"One brutal death is enough," Taggart said.

"I didn't mean to imply otherwise." Hugh placed the sausage on his appetizer plate beside a sliver of Gouda cheese. "I seem to recall that the young woman worked for Stanley and Abigail Preston. A shame about her accident."

The bodies had begun to pile up, and Hugh had cleverly implicated his coworker and friend, Stanley. As if to refute this bit of misdirection, Blake fastened a hard-edged stare at Hugh Waltham—the man responsible for this death and mayhem. Somewhere under that mask of cruelty, there must be a glimmer of decency and kindness that had drawn Jordan toward him and convinced her to marry the monster.

Blake watched as Hugh reached into a pocket in his fishing vest and took out a pocketknife with a buffalo horn handle. While talking about the unfortunate rise of violent crime in the city, he pulled out the long blade, probably four inches. Damascus steel, with a serrated edge near the hilt. Hugh sliced into his chorizo and lifted his gaze to return Blake's glare.

Brandishing the knife, a weapon that matched the scars on Jordan's wrists, was a direct challenge. The bastard thought he was bulletproof, and nobody could catch him.

Blake intended to prove him wrong. "Your ex-wife tried to investigate the murder of Bianca Hernandez," he said. "She mentioned that you helped her gather evidence."

"Another one of her causes," Hugh said as he cut

another slice of sausage. "Jordan always gravitated toward the underdog. Have you spoken to her recently?"

Blake kept his expression calm. "Have you?"

"She took the boys on vacation, but we didn't really speak."

"Do you know where she went?" Blake stretched out his long arm and took a slice of chorizo from Hugh's appetizer plate.

"Not really."

"I have a pretty good idea." Taggart leaned forward and held out the phone with the video of Jordan at the Magic Lamp. "That's her in Las Vegas with your pal, Caspar Khaled. She's kicking his butt."

Hugh looked away from the screen. "Jordan has a strange sense of humor."

"Doesn't look like a joke to me," Taggart said. "Last night, Khaled paid a visit to Rocky. And now you're here. Can you explain that coincidence?"

"Whatever my ex-wife does isn't my problem." He pointed the tip of his knife at Blake. "Maybe you should ask *him* where she is."

"Captain Delaney couldn't possibly have had anything to do with the death of Bianca Hernandez. He's been overseas."

"In the Middle East?" Hugh asked.

"I could tell you, but then I'd have to kill you." Blake hoped that his slow grin indicated how much he'd like to inflict grievous bodily harm on this scumbag. "Many of my missions were classified."

"Mine, too."

"In Congress, which is where you hope to work after the election, that's called a cover-up."

"What's it called for a marine?"

"My covert activity was done in the service of my country," Blake said. "I'm guessing that your secrets are to advance yourself and your bank account."

"What a shame." Hugh put away his blade. "I heard that you'll be retiring soon. You're no longer fit for battle."

I could take you with my eyes blindfolded and one hand tied behind my back. He wasn't surprised that Hugh knew the extent of his injuries. "I might be stationed in the Pentagon where I can keep an eye on people like you."

"If you're lucky, you might be standing guard outside the Oval Office."

"Another place you aspire to work," Blake said. So many elected officials set their sights on the highest office in the land. "You keep your eyes on the ultimate prize, and you don't allow anybody to get in the way."

Instead of backing down, Hugh leaned toward him. Blake stared back, but this was more than an old-fashioned contest to see who'd be the first to blink. Hugh was issuing a threat.

"I always win." Over his shoulder, he spoke to Rocky. "Isn't that right?"

The small man responded quickly. "Yes, sir."

"Any person—male or female—who tries to stop me will be sorry," he said. "He or she will lose everything, maybe even their life."

Blake clenched his fists to keep from strangling the man who sat with him at the table. Message received. Blake understood. Hugh would kill to reach his goal.

Bianca's murder was only the start. Abigail had also been eliminated. Jordan was next.

"Excuse me," Blake said as he rose to his feet. "Special Agent Taggart, I need to speak with you."

Taggart followed him out of the dining area and into the hallway. After a stop at the office where Taggart sent one of the other agents to keep an eye on Rocky and Hugh, Blake took SSA Taggart into the lavish bathroom with gold fixtures and a marble tub. Even after turning on multiple jets in the luxurious shower to cover the sound of their conversation, he kept his volume on extra low. Anybody could be listening with long-range devices or the whole house could be bugged.

"You heard him," Blake said. "Hugh admitted that he's going after Jordan. It's time for her and the kids to go to a safe house."

"Agreed," Taggart said. "I'll talk to Chester."

Blake took the cell phone from his pocket and spoke into it. "Jordan, are you there?"

"We're leaving your cabin and going to Chester's place." She adjusted her cell phone, so the screen showed her face. Her smile twitched nervously. "The boys just realized that it's almost Halloween. They couldn't care less about costumes, but they want the candy."

"How much of my conversation with Hugh did you hear?"

"Most of it. I wish I could have seen what was going on."

He thought of Hugh gesturing with the knife that had probably been used to slash her wrists and possibly to kill Bianca. He shuddered, glad that she hadn't witnessed Hugh's oversize ego in action. Jordan didn't need to be confronted with any other sick images. "Your ex-husband is an ass, but we have to take him seriously. He's dangerous. If he doesn't come after you, Khaled will. Or Gruber. It's time for you and the boys to go to a safe house."

"We're on the same page." Her head bobbed, setting her dark curls into motion. "Chester and I already talked about the safe house. He'll stay with the twins, so they'll have someone familiar. Put Taggart on the line so he can make arrangements with Chester."

"Wait," Blake said. "What about you?"

"I can't put the final pieces of my investigation together if I run away and hide. I'm so close, Blake."

Though he understood her feelings of ownership when it came to the evidence it had taken years for her to compile, he wanted her to step aside. "Please, Jordan. Go with the boys. Let the FBI handle this."

"I can't quit now."

His protective instincts surged. He doubted she would change her mind but made one more try. "Nobody is taking you off the case. You'll be informed every step of the way."

"I know how investigations work." She spoke with the authority of a reporter who had been embedded with the troops because she needed to see and experience the battles for herself. A secondary source wasn't good enough. "I'll be careful."

The best he could do was to stay by her side and keep her as safe as possible. Before he handed the cell phone to Taggart, he said, "Wait for me, Jordan."

The doctors who treated his recent injuries might

not think he was fit for duty, but Blake had to find the strength and skill for this mission. He had to guard this woman and defend her against the many people who wished to do her harm.

Chapter Eighteen

Seated at a Formica-topped table in the kitchenette of a nondescript motel suite in a small mountain town, Jordan stared into the plain white mug and wished she had something stronger than instant coffee to drink. When Chester and the twins took off in the FBI helicopter, leaving her behind in the shadow of gathering snow clouds, she'd kept grinning as she waved goodbye. Inside, she was sobbing hysterically. She wanted to scream. *Don't go. Stay with me.* But her children needed to be in a safe house, surrounded by high-level protection.

And she needed to stay.

The danger belonged to her alone. Her choice. She claimed it. After the FBI drove her to the motel, one of the agents offered to stay with her until Blake arrived, but she didn't need a babysitter. It was a point of pride— Jordan could take care of herself.

She pushed away from the small table, paced to the second-floor window and peeked out at the chilly scene outside from behind the edge of the closed curtains. Before he left, the agent had warned her about being too visible, and she agreed, mostly because she'd promised Blake that she'd be careful. As soon as she entered the room, she checked out the security. There were two exits. The door on this side of the room opened onto a concrete walkway. On the other side, she could step into a carpeted interior hallway. She'd added portable door locks to the standard-issue systems already in place. Not that her attempt to turn a motel suite into a fortress would be effective. The thugs who were after her could crash through a window or shoot off a lock.

If they wanted to get to her, they could. But why? Capturing her wouldn't make any difference in the FBI review of the evidence she'd already turned over. The best proof—hopefully the final proof—had to come from Rockwell's accounting records.

After all her digging, she had to ask herself if the investigation was worth the effort. A dream team of attorneys could help Hugh dodge those white-collar crimes and get off with a slap on the wrist. But the murder charge was a different matter, which was why she would see this investigation through to the end.

It was also why her ex-husband would do everything he could to get her out of his way.

The approaching danger cast a spotlight on the great dilemma of her life. *Who am I?* Oh damn, where to start? When she was younger, her dedication to her career took center stage. She chose her tiny, sparsely furnished apartment in New York because it was close to the newspapers and magazines that bought her articles. Decisions on her travel plans were dictated by headlines and breaking news. Her friends and associates came mostly from among the journalists, editors and investigators who she met on the job.

Even her relationship with Blake happened because she was working on an article. Her lover—former lover—represented the second phase in her life. She tapped her fingernail against the window. Where was he? Outside, she heard the slam of a car door and angled her neck so she could see who emerged from the unfamiliar Chevy sedan that slipped into a slot at the outer edge of the parking lot.

Watching and waiting, she felt like she was engaged in a weird version of Russian roulette. The man who got out of the car could be Gruber or one of his security guards. It might be an employee from the Magic Lamp. If she was lucky, she'd find herself looking down at Blake. It was him!

She recognized his knit watch cap with the US Navy logo, his wide shoulders, his towering height and his long strides as he mounted the staircase to the second floor. Blake carried a pizza box, which thrilled her almost as much as seeing him.

She unfastened the locks. One second after his bare knuckle rapped on her door, she whipped it open and pulled him inside. She kicked the door shut with a loud slam.

"About time," she said as she yanked the pizza box from his hands, dropped it on the desk near the door and tried to plaster herself against him. Something was in her way. "Ow, what's that?"

"My six-pack." He unzipped his parka, took out his six-pack and set it on the desk. "Got to have beer for pizza."

She gave him a long, hard kiss that literally took her breath away. Gasping, she stayed in his embrace, snuggled in the crook of his neck. A sense of belonging and longing enveloped her. This was exactly how things should be. She tilted her head back to peer into his eyes. "You changed my life, Blake. I've been thinking, and it's true. Before I met you, I was laser-focused on my journalism."

He tucked a curl behind her ear. "Before we talk, we need to lock the door."

"And then eat the pizza. What's on it?"

"Everything but anchovies."

Happiness bubbled through her like fizzy champagne. In this moment, she felt no fear from the menacing threat, no sadness at being separated from her boys and no anger at the injustice of crime. Only joy. The rest of the world faded away, and she lost herself in the pleasure of being held by a strong, good-looking man. Unable to hold herself back, she kissed him again.

As she watched him fasten the door locks, his every move seemed excellent and perfect. Whether driving a car or shooting a Glock, he'd always been skillful—the sort of man who could take care of whatever needed to be done. Her giddy observations went way over the top, but she couldn't stop herself. *Sweep me off my feet, Blake.* When he looked back at her and smiled, she desperately wanted to caress his jaw and kiss those endearing dimples.

In his gentle baritone, he asked, "How are the kids?"

"I wish you hadn't asked."

"Why not?"

She didn't want to return to reality, didn't want her fantasies to disappear. Not yet. She wanted to cling to the dream of being with him, covered in fairy dust and

rainbows. *What's wrong with me?* How could she forget about Alex and Cooper? The twins were the most
important people in her life, and she'd allowed them to
drop off her radar. *I'm a fool.* This must stop. She swiveled away from him, paced a few steps and sank onto
the edge of the bed.

"I'm not supposed to call them." Her voice fell flat,
devoid of tone or rhythm. "The FBI didn't think I was
being traced or monitored, but they didn't want to take
chances."

"What's wrong?" He sat beside her. His large hand
rested at the base of her neck and he lightly massaged.
"You look like somebody popped your bubble."

"Like I said, I was thinking about my life. First, I
was a journalist. Then I met you and had a taste of romance that left me wanting more."

"I did that?" His chest swelled. Proud of himself.

"*We* did that," she corrected. "It takes two. I don't
know if it was a matter of timing or hormones or fate,
but my world changed from harsh black-and-white to
gentle pastels."

This kiss was different. He took his time, and the
pressure of his lips against hers reminded her of the past
and, at the same time, gave a glimpse of what might
happen in the future. The veils of fear and anger swirled
in a capricious wind as her mood lightened. Still, she
pushed away from him.

"Again," he said, "tell me what's wrong."

"My life changed again when our romance ended.
I became a mom. My life had a new purpose. Those
first couple of years when the twins were babies, I was

overworked, exhausted, confused and terrified that I was doing everything wrong. I had never been happier."

He continued to stroke her back. "And who are you now, Jordan?"

"Trying to balance my journalistic instincts with being a full-time mother. And now, there's you. I'm juggling all these balls in the air, and I can't let any of them hit the floor." She turned her head and looked at him. "Am I being overdramatic?"

"A little bit." He held his thumb and index finger about an inch apart to indicate the small amount of drama. As she watched, he stretched the space wider and wider. "Maybe you're a diva reporter, like Brenda Starr or Lois Lane, but I like your grit."

"You advised me to walk away from the investigation and go to the safe house."

"I might have spoken too soon."

"You? Make a mistake?"

"It happens." He shrugged. "Seems to me that you can be all three. You can't stop being a mom. Why ignore your talent and training? You're good at digging for news stories like a rabid ferret. And that leaves romance. I think you can make time for me."

"I like that you made a list." She inhaled deeply, drawing in good vibes. "My obsessive habits are rubbing off on you."

"I'm beginning to understand how life works in Jordan's world. And I'm happy to volunteer for romance duty." He stood, took her hand and pulled her to her feet. "But first, we eat pizza."

"And drink beer."

While they chowed down, he told her about Taggart's

progress on the investigation. The FBI supervisory special agent had reprimanded the police officials in Flagstaff and demanded the cold case be reopened. "He ran through a whole series of crime scene details that needed to be sent to him and ordered the medical examiner to find a DNA match for Bianca's twin babies."

She washed down a savory bite of pizza with cold beer. "It's nice to have that kind of authority on an investigation. What's going to happen with Khaled?"

"His fate depends on Rocky. The squirrel is still denying any part in criminal activity, especially money laundering, but he's on the verge of taking a deal in exchange for testifying against his former employers."

She nibbled at the crust, her favorite part of the pizza. With the details of her investigation falling into place, she had second thoughts about not joining the twins at the safe house. "I have an emergency number for Taggart."

"So do I." Blake took a long swig of his beer. "There's something else I want to talk about. You and me and the romance we started seven years ago. You aren't the only one who thinks about those days. When I saw you hiking in the forest outside my cabin with the wind tangling in your hair and bringing out the roses in your cheeks, I went back in time. I was a healthy young man with my whole life ahead of me."

"You still are."

"I want to be the guy I was back then," he said, "in my prime. You deserve the best."

She wasn't sure she understood. "Have you looked in a mirror lately? You're not exactly a washed-up old hulk."

Instead of speaking, he stood, took off his belt holster

and placed his Glock on the bedside table within easy reach. He unfastened the buttons on his flannel shirt.

She cleared her throat. "What are you doing?"

He slipped off his shirt. Only the thin layer of a short-sleeved camouflage T-shirt covered his chest. "Ready?"

For what? She played along. "Yes."

He peeled off his T-shirt. His bare chest, lightly sprinkled with dark hair, displayed firm pecs and abs. And she saw his scars. Some were deep and puckered, ridges that tore across the muscles. Others faintly marked his skin and might, in time, fade to almost nothing. Hearing that he'd been badly injured had worried her but seeing the evidence made the explosion more real. She could almost feel his suffering. His buddy, Harvey from Henderson, had told her that the doctors didn't think he'd ever walk again. But Blake had recovered.

"I'm so proud of you," she said.

"Why?"

"Survival requires more strength and more courage than charging into battle."

She rose from her chair and came toward him. Her fingers traced the thickest scar that traversed his upper chest, where something had probably stabbed between his ribs and pierced his lung. Heat radiated from him. His flesh trembled under her touch, and his breathing became ragged. This response to her nearness delighted her and reflected her own pleasure. She saw his scars as medals of honor, evidence of his heroism and service.

When she pushed him down on the bed and started to climb on top of him, he caught hold of her arm. "Not like this," he said. "Take off your blouse."

Like him, the first item she removed was her physical protection in the form of the titanium baton fastened to her belt. The other layers—sweatshirt, blouse, T-shirt and bra—that kept her warm didn't make for a sexy striptease and took a while to remove. Finally, naked from the waist up, she straddled him, arched her back and flung her arms wide.

"I've changed, too," she said. "Giving birth and nursing twins can take a toll on a woman's body."

"You look good. Real good."

His gravel-voiced compliment teased her like a rough caress. When she slowly leaned down and joined with him, pressing her breasts against his chest, she felt fulfillment. The warmth from his large body was strong enough to keep an entire house cozy. The scars added an extra dimension. "I missed you."

He moved his hand along her spine, tapping her vertebrae like a xylophone. "I dreamed about you all the time, thought about you. Especially in the shower."

They had taken many fantastic showers together. "Why didn't you call?"

"You were busy, having another man's babies. And getting married to him."

"The wedding didn't happen until after the twins were born." She'd put off that final commitment for as long as possible. After the babies arrived, she wanted them to be part of their father's life. Worst mistake she'd ever made. "I'm lying in bed with you, Blake. The last thing I want to think about or talk about is my ex-husband."

This time, when their lips met, she tasted the pleasant tang of beer and pizza. His tongue penetrated her mouth and swirled, setting off a whirlwind of sensation. Her skin tingled. Her ears rang with the sound of his breathing.

He rolled her onto her back, and she put up zero resistance. But when he reached for the switch to turn off the lamp, she stopped him.

"I want to see what's going on," she said.

"It's too bright."

He was correct. The direct light wasn't conducive to the mood. "I'll fix it."

She darkened the room, except for the desk lamp. Then she tuned the radio to a smoky jazz station because a wailing saxophone and hot drumbeat were the best accompaniment for hot, hot sex. When she returned to the bed, she saw he'd made changes of his own. Obviously naked, he stretched out between the sheets.

In a few hasty seconds, she matched him by kicking off her sneakers and wriggling out of her jeans. As she snuggled beside him, his long legs tangled with hers. His muscular grasp overwhelmed her, and her brief struggle for control faded in utter capitulation. The best way to win this battle was by surrendering to his clever hands fondling her breasts. His fingers stroked the delicate flesh between her thighs. His lips kissed, and his teeth nipped.

He teased and teased. No man had ever aroused her the way Blake did. When he entered her, she was so very ready. Though she knew she'd felt this way before, seven years ago when they'd had sex for the first time, her climax felt brand-new.

With tremors racing through her body, she closed her eyes and accepted the incredible sensations that washed over her in wave after wave, predictable as the tide and equally miraculous. In the back of her mind, a tiny voice whispered. *Who am I?*

"I'm yours." Though unfeminist to think so, it was true. Blake owned a part of her that no one else would ever know.

"Did you say something?" he asked.

"Don't want to repeat it." She watched as he left the bed and went to the window. For a moment, she admired his back, scarred though it was along his spine. It was weird to stare at his bottom, but she couldn't look away. "What are you doing over there?"

He whipped the drapes open to reveal a thick, heavy snowfall against the black of night.

This storm brought more than high wind and heavy moisture. A blizzard. This would be a final test of their survival on Ice Mountain. Winter had arrived.

Chapter Nineteen

"I've changed my mind," Jordan said. "There's nothing more I can do for this investigation. It's time for me to give up and go to the FBI safe house."

Mindful of security, Blake closed the curtains and stalked across the motel room to the bed where she sat with pillows behind her back and the sheet tucked around her hips. Being naked with her had always been one of his favorite things. Jordan wasn't the least bit coy. In spite of what she'd said about the way her body looked after childbirth—which was, in his opinion, outstanding—she wasn't ashamed of her curves or the size of her perfect, round breasts. Her confidence enhanced her natural beauty.

He slid between the crisp, white sheets. This motel wasn't a five-star lodging, but the room suited their needs and didn't seem like the sort of place where Hugh would search for his ex-wife. Blake locked his gaze on her lovely face.

They had a lot more to talk about. "I'm sorry," he said.

"About what?"

"You can't go to the FBI house. Until Hugh is taken

into custody, the boys are more secure if you aren't near them."

She cocked her head to one side and stared at him. "I don't understand."

And he didn't want to explain. Instead, he'd rather dive under the covers and make love to her again and again until they were both too exhausted to move. He glided his hand along the smooth curve of her waist. "Maybe we should wait. We can talk in the morning."

"Now, we talk now." She slapped his hand away. "There's something you aren't telling me. Why can't I see my kids?"

"When you listened to my conversation at Rocky's dining room table with Hugh and Taggart, you didn't have the full picture. You couldn't see what was happening."

Clueless, she nodded. "Did Hugh pull a gun on you? Did he throw poison darts? What?"

Her ex-husband had given the appearance of civility. As a politician, he'd learned to mask all sorts of wrong behavior with the right moves and the right words. "We were eating cheese and sausage."

"I know. Hugh complimented Rocky on the charcuterie, an extra-fancy word for a common snack. Like referring to broccoli and carrots as crudités."

"He likes being extra fancy."

"Because he has no real taste." Her eyebrows pulled into a scowl. "He wouldn't mind if I dressed in garbage bags as long as they had designer labels. Tell me what happened."

"Hugh reached into a pocket on his fishing vest. And he took out a knife. It was a long blade, over four inches. Damascus steel, serrated at the hilt." He held her small hand in both of his. His thumb stroked the scar on her wrist. "The murder weapon."

Her eyelids fluttered as though trying to erase the picture he'd painted, but she couldn't escape the facts. The knife that killed Bianca belonged to Hugh. He was the murderer…which also meant he was the one who attacked her. As Blake watched her expression, he saw that realization dawning. She hadn't suspected him before now.

Three months ago, when she was abducted and taken to the Institute, she'd remembered Gruber zapping her with a stun gun and giving her an injection that knocked her unconscious. She'd assumed that her ex-husband's henchman slashed her wrists and nearly caused her to bleed to death. She hadn't seen the attack, but Hugh's knife had left the unusual scar.

"Unbelievable." Her voice faded to a sad whisper. "How could he? We were married. I'm the mother of his children."

Not a damned thing he said would ease her bone-deep disappointment and pain. Her ex-husband was evil, unredeemable. With a groan, she collapsed against Blake's chest. Her slender shoulders trembled, and her breathing came in ragged gasps. On some level, she must still have cherished memories of birthdays and Christmases when she and Hugh and the twins were a family. A good mother like Jordan couldn't help clinging to the hope that Alex and Cooper could have a decent relationship with their father.

He held her, trying to absorb some of her pain and waiting for the shock to subside. When she finally looked up at him, her enormous blue eyes were dry. No more tears for Hugh. Good. "He can't allow you to meet up with law enforcement," Blake said. "Three months ago, he turned you into the best evidence against him. You're the proof."

"The scars on my wrists match Bianca's wounds. Both were made by the same weapon. A knife that belongs to my ex-husband." A shudder went through her. "What if he throws it away? Or gives it to Gruber?"

"Taggart and I both saw the serrated blade. I'm guessing there are other witnesses. And photos from hunting or fishing trips."

"Still, Taggart should have seized the knife as material evidence."

"He didn't want to tip Hugh off."

"I don't like this strategy," she said. "Hugh's good at playing cat-and-mouse games."

"My money is on Taggart." This was a classic case of allowing an egomaniac enough rope to hang himself. "No way in hell is Hugh going to get away with this."

She left the bed, still naked, and went to the desk where her battered messenger bag rested on the floor beside the drawers. She took out a legal-size pad and a marker pen. "We need a plan."

Exactly what he expected her to say. He knew that Jordan would hold her rage, frustration and denial in check as long as she had a project to hold her focus. She wanted to get to work, to complete her investigation in spite of Hugh's minions, the casino thugs from the Magic Lamp and a snowstorm that promised to dump several inches overnight. "You make me proud," he said.

She thrust her arms into his plaid flannel shirt which was large enough to wrap around her small, slender body three or four times. Jordan had gone into planning mode and would ignore distractions. "First, we figure out the end goal."

Fortunately, he'd been paying attention when he was with Taggart. He leaned back against the pillows and folded his arms behind his head. "The FBI investigators, led by SSA Taggart, have been in touch with the federal prosecutors in Denver who have been reviewing the evidence."

"Any problem using illegally obtained evidence in their prosecution?"

"Some, but most of those federal legal eagles think you're brilliant."

Her lips stretched in a sly grin. "Because I am."

"They're putting together airtight cases against Hugh and some of his coconspirators. They're waiting for you. You're the final evidence. After you give a deposition, the whole gang will be charged and held pending indictment by a grand jury."

"But they'll still be eligible for bail," she said. "We won't be safe if Hugh makes bond and is released. The kids and I might be stuck in safe houses for a very long time."

"True enough." Blake wasn't a legal expert, but Taggart had answered this question for him. "On the charges of fraud, extortion and money laundering, they'll be able to get bail. But the brutal murder of a young, pregnant minor is different. Especially when it's compounded by the assault on you."

"And Abigail's supposed accident," she added.

Hugh's crimes almost qualified him for status as a serial killer. "A decent judge won't turn him loose after he reviews the evidence. No matter whether he's best friends with the President or not."

"How about Dr. Merchant?" she asked. "Will that quack be going to prison?"

"Taggart thought so." The psychiatrist had already returned to Flagstaff, but Khaled and his men were still in the Aspen area. "They're all going to pay."

"Just so you know, this isn't about revenge." She curled against the pillows beside him. "Well, maybe it's a little bit about revenge, but mostly I'm after justice. These men have done terrible things and need to be stopped."

He kissed the top of her head and inhaled the jasmine fragrance of her shampoo. "Tomorrow, we'll drive down to Denver and meet the prosecutor."

"Tomorrow?" She slapped her legal pad down on the bed. "Why wait?"

"I could tell you that it's because Hugh and Gruber are still combing the roadways, looking for us. Not to mention Khaled and his guys. There are a lot of people with vested interests in finding you and keeping you away from the federal prosecutor."

"Are you saying you're not up for a car chase over Independence Pass?"

"Not in Chester's Chevy Malibu. I mean, it's a great little car but not for high-speed pursuit."

"How did you end up with the Malibu?"

"Taggart and his men took Chester's Land Rover and Silverado. The zippy little car was all that was left."

"What about the Suburban?"

"It's at my cabin." He climbed off the bed, slipped into his jeans and returned to the window. This time, when he opened the curtain, the snow was blowing nearly horizontal. "That's a blizzard."

She stepped up beside him. "I didn't come this far to be defeated by weather."

"The reports I've heard predict six to twelve inches of snow and winds of more than thirty miles per hour. But the blizzard isn't supposed to last too long. Before noon tomorrow, it should slow down."

She turned away from the window. "I guess we're stuck here until morning."

"Sorry it throws a wrench in your plan." He tugged the curtain closed, took her hand and led her back toward the bed. "But it gives us a chance to finish the pizza and beer."

"Don't kid yourself, Blake. I have plenty more planning to do."

"Of course." He resigned himself.

"We need to map out a driving route," she said. "If all these bad guys are looking for us, we have to find an alternate way to get away from Ice Mountain."

He groaned, remembering their circuitous escape from Flagstaff. "Many of the roads aren't marked, and most of them feed into highways and central routes. Lucky for us, I've spent a lot of time up here in all sorts of weather."

"You know your way around."

"I do, but I've got to warn you. The back roads won't be plowed or cleared. It's slow going."

"Where do we start?" Her marker pen poised above the legal pad.

"Back to my cabin."

"The opposite direction from Denver."

This twisted logic only made sense if he looked at the big picture and visualized an old-fashioned map in his head. "There's a one-lane gravel road that zigzags over Ice Mountain Pass. It's not a great drive in any weather. Nobody will follow us there."

"And then?"

"Once I know we're safe, we contact Taggart. The FBI will give us a ride into Denver."

"Sensible."

"Really?"

She popped the lid back onto her marker and dropped it. "Let's make the feds our first option."

He was surprised that she was willing to give up so easily. "Is it strange for you to let somebody else take the lead?"

"Not a bit." She allowed the flannel shirt to slide off her shoulder, exposing her creamy skin. "I don't think of myself as a superheroine."

"You don't?" He bared her other shoulder.

"I need all the help I can get. There was a nurse at the Institute and an accountant who made sure I had the funds for my escape. Not to mention Emily Finnegan and her helicopter crew. And Spike. And dear Abigail." She exhaled a sigh. "And, of course, there's you."

"I like where this is headed."

Before they contacted Taggart in the morning, he had an excellent idea about how their time should be spent. When she gave him a wink and a slow, sensuous kiss, he suspected she was on the same page.

THE NEXT MORNING when Jordan stepped from her motel room into the grayish light of early morning, she might have been walking into a snow globe. Frigid winds tossed the fat, white flakes into swirling patterns. Heavy silence blanketed the parking lot. A plow had scraped off a layer and deposited the snow in a growing mountain beside the dumpster. The boughs of pine trees at the edge of the parking area were heavy with snow and bent low, almost touching the twelve inches that had fallen during the fierce overnight blizzard.

Gripping the handrail, she made her way to the concrete staircase at the far end. Though she wore gloves and a black knit cap with a pom-pom, she hadn't purchased snow boots for herself when she shopped for the kids. With every step, she regretted that oversight.

Blake had already moved the Malibu to the staircase. He'd brushed off the snow and started the engine to warm the interior. As she climbed inside and fastened her seat belt, she allowed herself to relax, which wasn't her usual state of mind at the start of a project. Being with Blake was good for her in so many ways. She could hardly believe it when she asked, "What should we do next?"

With his cheeks made ruddy from exposure, his blue eyes blazed. Snowflakes dusted the top of his cap. "Taggart wants us to meet him at a pancake house near his motel."

"Why didn't he stay here?"

"Bad weather. From the pancake house, he'll take care of our transportation problem."

Though she didn't like giving up the reins of control, she was relieved. Again. Getting to Denver and showing her scars to the prosecutor while being pursued by murderers and thugs was certainly a problem. But not her problem.

The nightmare investigation was almost over. From now on, all she had to do was show up and tell the truth. She had no reason to be on edge. And yet, when her super-encrypted cell phone buzzed in the pocket of her puffy jacket, her heartbeat accelerated. She was startled. An actual phone call. How odd! Spike usually sent text messages. It took her a while to dig out the phone and answer a number she didn't recognize.

"Who's this?" she demanded.

"Don't hang up. It's Caspar Khaled."

She stared through the windshield, then to the right and left as if she could see the bulky owner of the Magic Lamp standing on the street in his guayabera shirt with the white embroidery. The Malibu bumped over a curb as Blake drove onto the nearly vacant street outside their motel.

"How did you get this number?" she asked.

"Your buddy, Taggart. He has a leak."

"This must be a joke." Khaled ranked high among Hugh's friends. They worked together to defraud the IRS and the feds. She couldn't trust him. "I don't believe you."

"Listen, Jordan, I'm a businessman. At my casino, I sometimes skirt the law to save a buck, but I always play fair and give good odds."

"Why are you helping me?"

"Karma," he said. "I'm not a murderer. Not like Hugh."

She hated that he was making sense. "Go on."

"You're driving into a trap."

He disconnected the call and left her holding the cell phone. Could she believe him? The voice on her cell phone had sounded like Khaled and the karma comment was something he might say. If she trusted the caller, she and Blake needed to switch to her earlier plan, escaping by themselves and not looking back. Since they didn't know who among SSA Taggart's team had betrayed them, any contact was dangerous.

Or she might be overreacting. If the call was a ruse, she ought to ignore it and take her chances by joining the feds for pancakes and coffee.

An important decision loomed over her.

Against the pale sky, she saw the garish neon sign for Pancake Pete's. On the other side of the intersection, the headlights of two black SUVs glared at their spunky little Malibu. Those were the sort of heavy-duty vehicles Hugh preferred.

She turned to Blake. "We've got a change in plans."

Chapter Twenty

At her direction, Blake swerved wildly across the intersection and made a left turn, heading west. The rear tires of the Malibu sedan—not the world's best vehicle for maneuvering in snow—fishtailed on the frozen road as they drove past Pancake Pete's. In the parking lot, he saw the Land Rover that Taggart had been using and Chester's Silverado—a four-wheel drive vehicle he wished he was driving right now.

"Taggart has a leak," Jordan said as she twisted around in her seat to peer through the rear window. "Those two SUVs are following us. We almost drove into a trap."

"Who were you talking to?"

"Khaled." Before he could unleash a torrent of disbelief, she continued. "I don't think he's a good guy. You know that. But somebody believes in Khaled enough to give him my secret cell phone number. I'll send a text to Spike."

He didn't trust Khaled of the Magic Lamp as far as he could throw him, which wasn't far, given that the man had to weigh close to four hundred pounds. Still, Blake couldn't deny the presence of two SUVs with tinted windows that trailed their perky little Malibu. "What should we do next?"

"Do you remember the plan we made before we decided to meet with Taggart?"

Blake still had the map of obscure mountain roads in his head and was fully capable of engineering their escape from Ice Mountain. They made a good team— Jordan and him. She plotted the strategy and he handled the action. He pressed down on the accelerator and raised their speed to a level that wasn't remotely legal within city limits, especially not during a blizzard. "Hang on tight."

She made a nervous chirping noise, like the sound a chipmunk makes when it sights the approach of a predator. "Please don't kill us."

"It's okay. I'm good at this."

On the outskirts of town, there was almost zero traffic at a few minutes after seven o'clock on a weekday after a blizzard. If there hadn't been several inches of new snow clogging the road, he would have been speeding like a bullet. A heavy-duty truck with a snowplow attached to the front gave him an idea. He angled the Malibu around until he was directly behind the plow, riding on the newly cleared pavement.

Catching his breath, he glanced over at Jordan, who held her cell phone in a death grip and stared through the windshield with wild eyes. In a tiny voice, she said, "Are we still alive?"

"We're going back to Pancake Pete's."

"I don't think so. Taggart has a traitor on his team. We're better off on our own."

"Not to join up with the FBI." He reached down

and jingled the key chain in the ignition. Chester had a full set of keys for his house and for his other vehicles. "We're going to steal Chester's Silverado."

"Why?"

"This little Malibu isn't going to make it on the back roads. We need four-wheel drive. And a big V-8 engine." He offered no space for discussion. "I'll pull up next to the truck, and you jump in."

"You want me to run across an icy parking lot? In my sneakers?"

"It'd be better if you could fly, but I'll settle for running."

When he swung away from the path behind the snowplow, the Malibu was slowed by the accumulated snow on the road, and Blake knew he'd made the right decision. On the vacant roads, he skidded and twisted, barely maintaining control while he evaded the pursuing SUVs. In the center of a four-way stop intersection, he cranked the steering wheel and spun the Malibu in a three-sixty.

Jordan screamed as though she was in the front car of a roller coaster.

"I got this," he said.

"You don't." Another scream. "Let me out."

"Can't do that."

"Why not?"

Gunfire echoed through the snowy winter air.

"There's your reason," he said. Using every ounce of horsepower in the Malibu, he drove toward Pancake Pete's. While entering the parking lot, he had to slam on the brake and skidded sideways which he thought was an extremely cool move. Jordan shrieked again.

They were at the truck. He swung the car in a one-eighty so that her door was directly opposite the door to the passenger side of the truck. All she had to do was stagger a few steps and climb up into the cab.

He grabbed his satchel from the back seat, flung open his car door and ducked behind it while he returned fire. This wasn't the best place to make a final stand. He dashed around the rear of the Malibu, whipped open Jordan's door and ran to the opposite side of the truck to unlock the doors. As quickly as possible, he darted to the bed of the truck, crouched down and started shooting, drawing the gunfire from their pursuers. Out of bullets, he took another semiautomatic gun from his satchel and again returned fire. He distracted their attention. This was the moment for Jordan to make her move.

"Now," he yelled to her. "Get in the truck."

She screamed back at him. "I'm trying."

Help came from an unexpected direction. Blake saw Taggart and two other agents burst through the restaurant's glass doors. They moved in tactical formation, firing at the SUVs. The driver of one of the black vehicles with tinted windows gunned his engine and drove away.

"I'm in," Jordan yelled.

Blake vaulted into the driver's seat and fired up the engine. The muscular V-8 gave a deep, ferocious roar. Oh yeah, this was the vehicle he needed. "Jordan, are you okay?"

"Not shot. Not bleeding. Just go."

He threw the truck into Reverse and drove from the parking lot onto the road headed west. The studded tires gripped the pavement under the accumulated snow. Not exactly a smooth ride, but the truck handled the weather. Blake checked the rearview mirrors. "Nobody's following us."

"That was amazing." He heard the tremble in her voice. "Please, let's never do it again."

"You're shivering. Are you cold?"

"My sneakers are soaked through, and my feet feel like two ice cubes."

"Fasten your seat belt. I'm going to race up these steep curves into Ice Mountain." He relished the challenge. "And I'm fairly sure nobody has cleared the snow."

He dodged around a station wagon at a stoplight, muttering an apology under his breath that the other driver would never hear. Blake wouldn't have a chance to explain that he might appear to be a careless driver, but he was actually well trained in vehicular maneuvers and had been responsible for driving top-level diplomats through Beirut, Damascus, Abu Dhabi and Moscow.

He had a feeling that Jordan wouldn't be impressed with his explanation, either. She seemed to avoid looking through the windows by focusing intently on her cell phone. When her gaze flickered toward him, he asked, "You're okay, right?"

"It's better if I don't watch. Then I can't see that Volkswagen you're about to run into. Or those three guys on the curb. Or the bus. Oh, Blake, watch out for the bus."

"Might be useful if you kept an eye out for the SUVs."

"I've seen enough." She squeezed her eyes shut, then opened them. "I've seen too much. Behind the steering wheel in the SUV, I recognized Ray Gruber."

JORDAN STUDIED THE screen of her cell phone as though the mirrored surface was a crystal ball capable of predicting the future. Though she knew Gruber wasn't the person who slashed her wrists, he still scared her. He and Hugh's other security guards represented a mindless evil, dedicated to fulfilling her ex-husband's orders without question or pause.

"Gruber the Gorilla," Blake said.

"That's right." She looked up in time to see Blake hit the brake, swivel and turn into the skid. Her scream died before she had a chance to make a sound. An avid expression of delight crinkled the corners of his eyes. Though she found it hard to believe, he appeared to be enjoying himself.

Slouched in her seat, she stamped her feet on the floorboards to get the circulation going. The heater in the truck was turned on but would take a while to get going. She didn't expect a luxury ride, and she certainly wasn't going to complain. How could she do anything but appreciate Blake's ability to adapt quickly to a change in circumstance? He'd been prepared.

"Where did you get the weapons?" she asked.

"I told you about the gun safe at my cabin. With mobs of thugs coming at us, it seemed wise to have some firepower."

"Absolutely. And where did you learn those really annoying skills in evasive driving techniques? Is that a marine thing?"

"It's a guy thing."

He merged onto the highway. When she dared to peek over the dashboard, she saw a long stretch of road with no other cars. He was driving fast, probably too fast, but she wouldn't complain. The farther they got from Gruber and the gang, the better. After a half hour, the heater in the truck was beginning to have an effect. Though still cold, her toes didn't feel frostbitten.

Comfortable enough to sit up, she glanced over at him. "Did I thank you for saving me?"

"I think you did. Right after you accused me of trying to kill you."

Her phone rang. Again, she didn't recognize the number. "Who's this?"

"Your favorite computer geek." Spike cackled. "And you're so very welcome."

He spoke with an unidentifiable, oddly flowery accent that could have been French or Swahili. Long ago, she'd given up trying to figure out where he was from or where he was going. She put the call on speakerphone. "What am I supposed to be thanking you for?"

"Caspar Khaled. I daresay we misjudged the fellow. When you confronted him in Vegas, what was your impression of him?"

"I thought he was going to eat me."

"Hah!" In the background, she heard the tappity-tap of computer keys. She wasn't sure Spike was human. He could just as easily have been a robot. "Khaled is working with the feds. If he'd captured you, he would have protected you from your ex-husband."

"I'm confused." When had Khaled joined the good guys? How could Taggart have a traitor in his midst? More important, who was it? "Which agent turned against us?"

"Not sure. Steer clear of them, all of them."

"Even SSA Taggart?" She looked toward Blake,

who was listening while he drove the curving mountain roads with only one hand on the wheel. "Can we trust him?"

"Not to put too fine a point on your plans, my dear Jordan, but trust is not an issue. You have only one job. One project. One plan."

She nodded. "Go to Denver and meet with the federal prosecutor, Orville Peterson."

"Correct," Spike said. "Tell me where you are right now."

Blake spoke up. "We're about a mile from my cabin, which means we're three miles from the old road that runs along the north ridge of Ice Mountain."

She groaned. They'd driven that way before. It was a trail that hugged the side of a cliff on one side and had a sheer drop of hundreds of feet on the other. "Is there another route?"

"You had better find one," Spike said. "If you follow the ridge, you'll run smack-dab into one of those SUVs."

"How do you know that?" Blake asked.

"I hacked their GPS systems," Spike said. "And don't even think of going backwards. The second SUV is following you. And they're getting closer."

Her computer geek was odd but really good at what he did. "Suggestions?" she asked.

"Circle the lake. There's another route on the far side of Chipmunk Creek. It will take you miles in the wrong direction, but I don't see another way."

"Thanks for the help," Blake said. "Keep us posted on the whereabouts of the bad guys."

She disconnected the call with Spike. As soon as

she'd heard that they needed a new route, her brain started ticking. "I have a plan."

"Why am I not surprised?"

"This might not be brilliant, but it's better than driving aimlessly around the lake, hoping we won't run into Gruber and the boys." She leaned forward and peered through the upper portion of the windshield. "Colorado weather is incredible. The blizzard is over. And the sun is trying to break through."

"I've seen days when the temperature changed forty degrees in one afternoon."

"We should take advantage."

He gave her a curious look. "Okay."

"We fly."

As far as she knew, there was still a chopper at Chester's house. She knew how to fly a helicopter and so did Blake.

She'd come up with this plan just in time. When they drove past his cabin without stopping, she caught a glimpse of the SUV following them. Blake guided the truck off the two-lane road onto the narrow path that led down to the lake. Apparently, he had a plan of his own. "Where are we going?"

"Before we fly, we swim. Not literally, but we can elude the guys behind us by using Chester's little red motorboat. It's still tied at the pier."

Not a choice she would have made, but it was a good plan. When he parked the truck, she had to force herself to leave the warm cab of the truck. The accumulated snow on the ground rose higher than her ankles. *So cold.* She staggered through it, lurching toward the short, wooden pier. Blake came up behind her and pressed the keys into her palm.

"It's the metallic red one."

"Of course it is."

In his left hand, he held a short semiautomatic. With his right, he pulled her close and kissed her hard. Then he raised the barrel of his weapon and aimed at the SUV that came to a stop behind the truck.

She tiptoed along the pier as fast as she could without slipping. If she could make it to the boat without falling, she was halfway there. If not…there were worse ways to die than drowning in ice-cold water.

Chapter Twenty-One

After the IED explosion that seriously damaged his career in the marines, Blake hadn't expected to ever find himself in a combat situation again. Firefights and shoot-outs weren't a regular part of most people's lives. But right now, his training and experience as a sharp-shooter came in handy, and he was armed with a semi-automatic Remington, an outstanding weapon with an excellent hunting scope.

Three men emerged from the SUV with guns drawn. Gruber joined them. From where they stood on the snow-covered hill above the truck, they might be able to see Jordan creeping along the icy pier but wouldn't be able to get a good shot at her. Blake fired a warning into the air, and the security men scattered.

Hiding behind the SUV, Gruber yelled, "Nobody has to get hurt."

"Correct," Blake responded. "You're free to go."

"Give up, Mr. Marine. You're outgunned and out-manned."

"That's Captain Marine to you."

In the exchange of gunfire, Blake disabled one man and scared the others. He avoided kill shots. No reason these fools had to die for their employer. Blake's purpose was to hold them off, to keep them away from the pier until he and Jordan could make their escape.

Glancing over his shoulder, he saw her in the cockpit of the little red boat. Though the boat was still moored to the dock, she engaged the starter. The engine sputtered once, twice and then it died. *Come on, baby, let's go.* Chester was the kind of guy who kept his equipment in peak condition. The damn boat would start. It had to start.

Though Gruber kept himself shielded, his men took risks. Blake nailed one of them in the thigh—not a lethal wound but enough to make him fall.

From the pier, he heard the reassuring hum of the motor. After another few shots, he retreated down the slope through the snow. Dodging through the trees, he paused every few steps, braced his rifle, peered into the scope and fired.

"Hurry," Jordan yelled.

"Take cover. Get down."

The snow on the wooden pier had already started to melt, but the surface remained slippery. It took forever for him to reach the boat, untie the hitch and climb into the back. He faced the hill where the SUV and truck were parked. The shots he fired as Jordan pulled away kept Gruber and his men at bay.

With Jordan at the wheel, the little red motorboat sliced across the smooth, tranquil water. The blizzard wind from last night had calmed, and the clouds in the eastern sky had begun to fade. Blue skies gave him fresh hope. He slipped into the seat beside her. "Do you want me to drive?"

"It's all yours, Captain." She shivered and leaned away from the edge of the boat where droplets of spray stabbed into them like icy pinpricks. "I've never been so cold."

A surge of adrenaline had caused his heart to race and his breathing to accelerate. Under his parka, he was actually sweating. But he knew that as soon as the rush played out, he'd be hit by the cold. "Tonight, we'll stay in a hotel, maybe soak in a hot tub."

"Heavenly." She wrapped her arms around her middle. "When we get into the chopper, I'm taking my frozen sneakers off."

"Almost there."

"Already?"

"That's Chester's place over there. I'm sure because not many people have a helicopter in the front yard." Lucky for them, the chopper had been swept clean of snow and deiced. The pilot must have already been out this morning. "It'll take Gruber and his pals a half hour or more to maneuver their SUV out of the snowbank where they're parked and get over here. But we should still hurry. I don't trust the weather."

"Or the FBI," she said.

He guided Chester's boat to the pier, secured it and took her hand to help her come ashore. "It just occurred to me that I never asked if you could handle a motorboat."

"I learned in high school in Boston. And don't forget, I can also fly a chopper. Emily taught me the basics."

She latched onto his arm as they walked up the wooden pier to the shore, and he liked feeling that he was her protector. "I'll go up the hill to the cabin and find the pilot. No reason for you to make that hike. Wait for me by the bird."

Before he moved away from her, she caught hold of his arm and pulled him back toward her. On the other side of the lake, he'd given her a kiss for luck. Now it was her turn. Her lips were soft. In spite of what she'd said about being cold, her body radiated heat. Though tempted to stay right there and do much more than kiss, he stepped back and pivoted. "I'll get the pilot."

Over his shoulder, he saw her take her phone from her pocket and answer the buzz of an incoming call. Halfway up the hill to Chester's cabin—which was ten years older than his with twice the square footage—he heard her calling to him. He turned and saw her frantically waving her arms.

"What's wrong?" he shouted.

"Don't go into the cabin."

That didn't make any sense. "Why not?"

"This is Spike. He says it's booby-trapped."

Spike had been a reliable source of information who hadn't steered them wrong. But if the cabin was rigged with a bomb, where was the pilot? Blake noted several sets of footprints in the snow between the cabin and the helipad. What the hell was going on?

The air surrounding him felt heavy and intense as though dark foreboding had swallowed the blue-sky hope. The concussive force of the explosion hit him before he heard the earsplitting blast and was knocked onto his back. Desperately, he tried to get up but couldn't move. Fierce orange flames and trails of black smoke leaped high into the air. He saw more than snow, sky and trees. Transported back in time to a different explosion. His vision filled with images of the men, his friends, who nearly died beside him on a lonely road in the Middle East. He saw their bodies, torn and bleeding.

His eyes closed. Remembered pain held him in a steel grip.

In the analytical part of his brain, he recognized the symptoms. Seeing people who weren't there. Feeling sensory images that obscured reality. He couldn't move. His limbs were frozen. He was experiencing a flashback but couldn't stop it from happening.

STUNNED, JORDAN GAPED at the burning cabin. The front door had been incinerated and the roof caved in. The logs were charred. The deck, destroyed. She didn't think Blake had been close enough to be injured by flying debris, but he wasn't moving. If he'd been hurt, it was her fault, just like Abigail.

She struggled up the snow-covered hill toward him, fighting her way through the freezing snow. The cell phone in her hand rang again, and she held it to her ear.

"Jordan," Spike said. "Are you all right?"

"It's Blake. He's not moving."

"You've got to get him out of there. It's up to you."

"What about the pilot?" she asked. "What if he was inside the cabin?"

"He's the traitor."

The enormity of what he'd said hit her like an avalanche. The pilot had taken the twins to the safe house. She'd had a call from Chester yesterday to let her know they were all right, but the pilot knew their location. "Did he set the bomb?"

"Likely," Spike said. "Later, you can investigate. Right now, help Blake and get the hell out of there."

"I owe you, Spike."

"Correct." He ended the call.

She staggered the last few steps and sprawled in the snow beside Blake. He had turned on his side with his shoulders hunched and his face covered with one hand. The heat from the explosion reached across the grounds and touched her. She welcomed the warmth and despised the destruction.

Reaching out, she touched his back. "Blake, are you okay?"

Lightning fast, he flipped onto his knees and lunged at her. His right hand shot toward her, and he grasped her throat in a stranglehold. The pupils of his eyes were so dilated that she could barely see the blue of his irises. Though looking directly at her, he wasn't seeing her. The explosion had triggered his trauma.

"Blake." She choked out his name. "It's me, Jordan."

He blinked and pulled his hand away from her. "What have I done?"

"We've got to get away from here before Gruber catches up." She rose to her feet and pulled him with her. "Come with me. We're going to the helicopter."

"The pilot. He wasn't in the house, was he?"

"He's the traitor. We have to let Taggart know."

He straightened his spine. Though she couldn't see any sign of injury on him, he moved with a severe limp and held his left arm at a strange angle. His body seemed to be reliving the wounds he received when the IED exploded, similar to phantom limb syndrome where the patient feels pain in an arm or leg that has been amputated.

Though he leaned on her for support, she didn't have the strength to carry him. Blake was twice her size. When he paused to catch his breath, she urged him forward. For a moment she considered taking his rifle, but it was too much to carry. "We're almost there."

"Go without me. You need to get into Denver."

"Don't be a jerk."

"What?"

"I'm not leaving you behind." In spite of his trauma, she roared. Now wasn't the time for nobility. They needed to survive. "You give me hope. You're my reason to keep going."

"Me and the twins?"

"Yes." She dragged him the last few steps to the helicopter.

"Marry me, Jordan."

That declaration would have meant a lot more if he hadn't been half-unconscious. She forced him into the chopper where he crumpled into a heap behind the pilot's seat. The controls for this bird were a lot more complicated than Emily's smaller sightseeing helicopter, but Jordan thought she could handle it. There was no other choice.

Behind her shoulder, she heard a sound and turned. A man separated from the shadows at the rear of the fuselage. Her ex-husband came at her.

She dodged his grasp. "I should have taken the rifle."

"Shoulda, coulda, woulda." His trademark white smile glistened—a horrible contrast to the flames of the explosion that she could see through the open side door of the chopper. "There are so damn many things you should have done differently."

"Starting with our marriage."

"I'd have to agree," he said. "But let me remind you how happy you were when the twins were born. They're good boys. Handsome and smart. When I run for office, it'll look good to have them standing beside me. My poor, motherless children."

"You'll never get away with this. The fire department will respond."

"Gruber will be here before anybody else. We'll drive away. It's over. My problem will be eliminated." He reached into this pocket and pulled out his distinctive knife. "I should have killed you the first time I had the chance."

She drew her titanium baton. With a flick of her wrist, it opened to the full twenty-six inches. The cramped space in the chopper worked to her advantage. She was smaller with more room to move. Hugh was clumsy, had always been clumsy.

"One question," she said. "Did you kill Abigail?"

"Nosy bitch." He made a wide sweep with his blade. "I mentioned to her hubby that she was a problem, and good old Stanley arranged the car accident. He'd been planning her death for months."

"Do all of your friends kill their wives?"

"Only the first wife."

She whipped her baton and hit his upper arm. He made a grab for her weapon but missed. She positioned herself again. "Ouch, that's going to leave a bruise. Maybe you ought to call for backup. Where's the pilot?"

"He became a problem—wanted too much money for the payoff. I assume he died in the explosion."

"You're a ruthless son of a bitch."

"That might be the sweetest thing you've ever said to me."

He charged. Her only escape was to hit the floor in the chopper and roll, but there wasn't room. She was in trouble.

From behind the seats, Blake staggered to his feet and unzipped his parka. "It's over, Hugh."

He barked a laugh. "You can barely stand up. She's a bigger threat than you are."

"But I have a gun."

When he reached for his side holster and pulled out his Glock, Jordan almost cheered. He was her man— always prepared.

"Drop the knife," he said.

As soon as Hugh disarmed himself, Jordan grabbed that important piece of evidence. The murder weapon. She chuckled. "You know what they say. Never bring a knife to a gunfight."

"He's not that stupid," Blake said. "I'm sure he's got other hidden weapons, but we don't have time to mess around with this criminal. You have a choice, Hugh. You can jump out the side door or I can shoot you and push your lifeless body to the ground. Either way, Jordan and I are taking off in twelve seconds."

Hugh jumped.

"Why twelve?" she asked.

"Sounded good." He took the pilot's seat and handed her the Glock. "If Hugh comes at us, shoot him."

"Why didn't you pull the trigger?"

"That's Taggart's job. I'm out of the lethal force business."

In slightly more than twelve seconds, they took off. Above the cloud cover, the skies were blue and the sun was shining.

She spoke into the headset. "Do you remember proposing to me?"

"I love you, Jordan."

"My answer is yes." She'd have to talk to the twins but was sure they'd approve. "And I love you back."

Finally, the nightmare was over. She looked forward to planning the wedding. Even more than that, she was ready to live happily ever after.

SIX MONTHS LATER, Jordan made the final arrangement for a small ceremony in the landscaped backyard of the house she and Blake had purchased in Richmond, Virginia, which was not far from where Blake had taken a job at the Pentagon. Grudgingly, he'd discovered that he liked working at a higher level, determining policy while always looking out for the men and women who served in the Corps.

Hugh and his minions, including Stanley Preston, who was involved in the murder of his wife, Abigail, were awaiting trial. The final evidence against Hugh came when the medical examiner found the "lost" DNA results for Bianca's unborn babies. A match for Hugh, the DNA was a solid motive for murder.

Jordan returned to the living room through the French doors and stood for a moment, enjoying the presence of family, old friends and acquaintances. Emily Finnegan from Vegas hadn't hooked up with Harvey from Henderson but fixed him up with a friend of hers. Bianca's sister had gone back to school. The nurse who had helped Jordan escape from the Gateway Institute met up with Spike, a classy-looking Englishman, who sat at the upright piano and played "Bohemian Rhapsody" while the twins sang along with wildly inaccurate lyrics. They were coached by her mom, in from Boston, and Chester, who made a great couple.

Though all these friendships fulfilled her, there was still something missing from Jordan's life. She didn't know exactly what it was until she answered a phone call from Hornsby. Her former mentor had an assignment for her that involved a serial killer in the wilderness country of Utah.

She made her decision in less than five seconds. "I'm on it."

As she ended the call, she looked up and saw Blake, resplendent in his dress blues, descending the staircase. His trimmed blond hair had picked up a few strands of silver, which made it shine. And his fierce blue eyes made tender contact with hers.

Now, her life was perfect.

* * * * *

Look for more books from USA TODAY
*bestselling author Cassie Miles coming soon from
Harlequin Intrigue!*

And don't miss her most recent book,
Gaslighted in Colorado, *available now wherever
Harlequin Intrigue books are sold!*

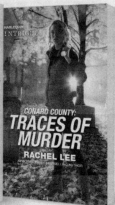

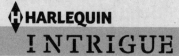

SPECIAL EXCERPT FROM

(H) HARLEQUIN

INTRIGUE

Read on for a sneak peek at
Christmas Ransom,
the third book in New York Times *bestselling author*
B.J. Daniels's *A Colt Brothers Investigation series.*

The whole desperate plan began simply as a last-ditch attempt to save his life. He never intended for anyone to get hurt. That day, not long after Thanksgiving, he walked into the bank full of hope. It was the first time he'd ever asked for a loan. It was also the first time he'd ever seen executive loan officer Carla Richmond.

When he tapped at her open doorway, she looked up from that big desk of hers. He thought she was too young and pretty with her big blue eyes and all that curly chestnut-brown hair to make the decision as to whether he lived or died.

She had a great smile as she got to her feet to offer him a seat.

He felt so out of place in her plush office that he stood in the doorway nervously kneading the brim of his worn baseball cap for a moment before stepping in. As he did, her blue-eyed gaze took in his ill-fitting clothing hanging on his rangy body, his bad haircut, his large, weathered hands.

He told himself that she'd already made up her mind before he even sat down. She didn't give men like him a second look—let alone money. Like his father always said, bankers never gave dough to poor people who actually needed it. They just helped their rich friends.

Right away Carla Richmond made him feel small with her questions about his employment record, what he had for collateral, why he needed the money and how he planned to repay it. He'd recently lost one crappy job and was in the process of starting another temporary one, and all he had to show for the years he'd worked hard labor since high school was an old pickup and a pile of bills.

He took the forms she handed him and thanked her, knowing he wasn't going to bother filling them in. On the way out of her office, he balled them up and dropped them in the trash. All the way to his pickup, he mentally kicked himself for being such a fool. What had he expected?

No one was going to give him money, even to save his life—especially some woman in a suit behind a big desk in an air-conditioned office. It didn't matter that she didn't have a clue how desperate he really was. All she'd seen when she'd looked at him was a loser. To think that he'd bought a new pair of jeans with the last of his cash and borrowed a too-large button-up shirt from a former coworker for this meeting.

After climbing into his truck, he sat for a moment, too scared and sick at heart to start the engine. The worst part was the thought of going home and telling Jesse. The way his luck was going, she would walk out on him. Not that he could blame her, since his gambling had gotten them into this mess.

He thought about blowing off work, since his new job was only temporary anyway, and going straight to the bar. Then he reminded himself that he'd spent the last of his money on the jeans. He couldn't even afford a beer. His own fault, he reminded himself. He'd only made things worse when he'd gone to a loan shark for cash and then stupidly gambled the money, thinking he could make back what he owed and then some when he won. He'd been so sure his luck had changed for the better when he'd met Jesse.

Last time the two thugs had come to collect the interest on the loan, they'd left him bleeding in the dirt outside his rented house. They would be back any day.

With a curse, he started the pickup. A cloud of exhaust blew out the back as he headed home to face Jesse with the bad news. Asking for a loan had been a long shot, but still he couldn't help thinking about the disappointment he'd see in her eyes when he told her. They'd planned to go out tonight for an expensive dinner with the loan money to celebrate.

As he drove home, his humiliation began to fester like a sore that just wouldn't heal. Had he known even then how this was going to end? Or was he still telling himself he was just a nice guy who'd made some mistakes, had some bad luck and gotten involved with the wrong people?

Don't miss
Christmas Ransom *by B.J. Daniels,*
available December 2022 wherever
Harlequin books and ebooks are sold.

Harlequin.com

Love Harlequin romance?

DISCOVER.

Be the first to find out about promotions,
news and exclusive content!

Facebook.com/HarlequinBooks

Twitter.com/HarlequinBooks

Instagram.com/HarlequinBooks

Pinterest.com/HarlequinBooks

YouTube.com/HarlequinBooks

ReaderService.com

EXPLORE.

Sign up for the Harlequin e-newsletter and
download a free book from any series at
TryHarlequin.com

CONNECT.

Join our Harlequin community to
share your thoughts and connect
with other romance readers!
Facebook.com/groups/HarlequinConnection

HARLEQUIN

Heartfelt or thrilling, passionate or uplifting—Harlequin is more than just happily-ever-after.

With twelve different series to choose from and new books available every month, you are sure to find stories that will move you, uplift you, inspire and delight you.